E, MY NAME IS
Emily

E, MY NAME IS
Emily

NORMA FOX MAZER

AN
APPLE
PAPERBACK

SCHOLASTIC INC.
New York Toronto London Auckland Sydney

ISBN 0-590-43654-6

12 11 10 9 8 7 6 5 4 3 2 1   9   4 5 6 7 8 9/9

Printed in the U.S.A.   40

For my niece
Lucy Northrop —
also a friend

Chapter 1

As soon as I got off the school bus I heard my best friend, Bunny Larrabee, calling me. "Emily, Emily!" I peered around for her. I'm nearsighted. Dr. Weiss says I should wear my glasses all the time, but I hardly ever do. I don't like the way I look in them, but it's not just vanity. I have a theory that the less I use my glasses, the more my eyes will improve from the muscles being forced to work. In the meantime, though, I have to admit that anything more than five feet away is kind of blurry.

"This way," Bunny was yelling. "Over here, Emily." Just as I finally located her in the crowd of kids, she ran toward me and grabbed my arm. "Emily, look at us!"

"Oh, no!" We were wearing practically identical outfits, flowered jeans, black cotton sweaters, and black boots.

"I can't believe this," Bunny said. "I went for these clothes half asleep; I didn't even *think* about what I was going to wear."

"I did." I'd stayed in bed ten minutes after the alarm, figuring out my clothes exactly. Of course, being best friends, it wasn't the first time we'd ever come to school dressed alike. We used to do it all the time when we were in the sixth and seventh grade, but at least then it was planned.

"Well, our earrings are different, anyway," I said. I was wearing dangly purple bead earrings that I'd bought on sale. Bunny had on the Guatemalan ones her father had given her after one of his trips. They were handmade little knitted dolls in native costume: a tiny man in her left ear and a tiny woman in her right ear.

"Let's braid my hair," Bunny said as we went up the stairs into the building.

"Then we really will look like twins." I'd done my hair in a single braid down my back, with a bow at the top.

"I should only be so lucky. You gorgeous thing!"

I blushed. Bunny is always doing that, talking as if I'm a beauty queen or something. Even though I'm aware that it's just her way of building me up, building my confidence, it sort of works. When I'm with her, I do feel much prettier than usual.

In the girls' room, I started brushing and braiding her hair. It's thick and honey-colored. Mine is sort of wispy and dark. I like her hair much better.

"Did you watch Meridith Finkle's show last night?" Bunny sighed. "If I could ever be one tenth as funny!"

Bunny wants to be a clown or a comedian. She has a million jokes and a rubber face. I think she's going to be famous someday.

"I love her voice and the way she walks and everything about her. Her timing is exquisite. . . . I wanna grow up to be Meridith Finkle!" she honked in a flat voice, just like Meridith Finkle's.

I laughed. "You'll have to get fat first."

"Oh, don't say it!" She puffed out her cheeks. "Shad made fudge last night. My whole diet down the drain. Now I'll have to be extra good all week."

Shad is Bunny's nine-year-old brother. She also has an older sister, Star, who's away at college studying physics. They're all smart in that family, but Shad is so smart, I think he might get to college before either Bunny or me.

"I was eating my fudge and I was eating Shad's fudge," Bunny went on. "I couldn't stop.

3

I had a fudge hunger, a fudge craving, a fudge obsession. Shad got so mad he tried to beat me up." She snickered. "That skinny little pacifist didn't know who he was tangling with."

Bunny went on talking, but suddenly I sort of blanked out. Did you ever have that happen to you? Someone innocently says a word, and all at once there's this moment from the past in your mind that pushes everything else away. It was the word *tangle* that did it. That, plus braiding Bunny's hair, I think, because the memory was about braiding: my father combing and braiding my hair one morning about seven years ago.

It was so strange. There I was, in the girls' bathroom, calmly pulling one strand of Bunny's hair over the other, and yet I seemed to be *there*, too, back in the living room of our old house on Oak Street. The feeling was so vivid my cheeks got hot, my whole face flared up.

In my mind I could see little things like a crumpled tissue on the floor near the brown couch and a loose thread on my father's sweater, and I could feel the boniness of his knee as I leaned against him. I heard him calling me *Miss Tangles* and saying that Mom wasn't out of bed yet, so he'd braid me this morning. And I remembered how I was convinced my father was the tallest man in the world and the nicest and definitely the most fun.

"My hair doesn't look good this way, Em,"

4

Bunny said. "We gotta take it out."

Her voice startled me. My stomach jumped. It was like being awakened from a dream. As suddenly as it had come, the memory, the whole thing, the *realness* of it was gone.

"You can wear a braid, Em, because you've got great bones," Bunny was saying, "but pulling my hair back makes my front teeth look even huge-er." She started yanking out the braid. "I hate these teeth! They stick out."

"They do not." I pushed her hands away from her hair. "Let me do that, you're making a mess. . . . Did I ever tell you how my father used to make up songs for me?"

"Only about a million times. And my teeth *do* too stick out. It's the curse of my life."

"I remember one he used to sing. *'Frogboy is comin' to visit Emilybird, ooh la ooh la, bring her some green guggy food, ooh la ooh la . . .' "*

Bunny looked at me in the mirror. "Pardon me if I don't comment; I don't want to insult your father's talent. I like him too much. Remember when he took us up in the balloon?"

I nodded. "He never writes," I said.

"Oh, Em, don't start getting depressed."

"He never calls, either."

"When my father goes away on a trip, he doesn't write or call, either."

"My father's not away on a trip, Bunny."

First bell rang. Bunny put her arm through

5

mine. "Smile. Or I'll have to tell you a joke." I forced my lips up. "You gotta do better than that," Bunny said. "I see a joke is needed here."

"Bunny, shut up, please." Why couldn't I just be gloomy and depressed if that's the way I happened to feel?

"Did you hear what the ceiling said to the wall?"

"Nooo."

"Hold me up, I'm plastered."

"Drunk joke, ugh."

"A guy spent thousands of dollars to have his family tree checked out . . . he discovered that he was a sap."

"Bun-ny." But I laughed that time. "That was a terrible joke. I laugh at anything."

"You are my best audience," she admitted.

I dug into my sack and pulled out a copy of *Great Bones*, the book I'd finished reading last night. "You have to read this."

"Who's the cute guy on the cover?"

She always wanted to know that. "You're going to love this one. There's one part in there that's so hilarious, where the girl says, 'My name is Jan Bones. Call me Jan or call me Bones.' "

Bunny looked at me, raising her eyebrows. "That's as funny as it gets?" She flipped through the pages. "Any hot scenes?"

"A few."

"How far do I have to read to get to them?"

"On page fifty, they kiss — "

"Fifty! Not before that?"

"Bunny, it's worth the wait. When they kiss, it's so romantic. When I read that part, I could imagine myself being Jan. They're near a waterfall and I could practically hear the water, and it was like I was Jan — "

"You have a great imagination, Em."

" — and I was trying to tell him I wanted him to kiss me."

"What do you mean, you *wanted* him to — I thought you said they *did* kiss."

"They did, but first she had to convince him." I stuffed the book in her knapsack. "Promise you'll read it this weekend."

"I'll read it, I'll read it."

Chapter 2

I hate Sundays. We all just hang around the house. Mom acts tired. The twins fight. And I do homework. "I can't think of an opening for this essay," I said. "Does anyone want to help me?"

It was almost suppertime, but the lunch dishes were still on the table. I cleared a space for myself at one end. The twins had been playing Monopoly until Wilma got mad because Chris was winning. Now she was in the living room, shrieking over her favorite TV show. I call it Stupidest Home Videos. What's so funny about a woman getting her head stuck in a toilet? Or a man on a ladder with his pants falling down?

Chris was lying on his back in the middle of

the kitchen floor, playing with his Original Melted Snowman paperweight. Dad gave it to him ages ago. Inside the glass are a tiny black hat and two carrots floating in water. Get it? We're all fairly sick of the joke, but Chris won't go anywhere without the Original Melted Snowman.

Did I say my sister and brother were twins? Not identical, naturally. Fraternal. Two eggs. "Two *very different* eggs," Mom says. Chris is like her, slow and sort of dreamy. I think I'm like my father, but Wilma is just — Wilma! "She's a force of nature," Bunny says.

"Can someone help me with this essay?" I repeated. I meant my mother. She can have good ideas about writing. She got A's in college. But right now she had her head stuck in the refrigerator — like another scene from Stupidest Home Vidcos! Lately, she irritates me a lot. The way she doesn't finish her sentences. And the way she dresses. She'll go outside to wash the car or get the newspaper in anything, even her green running pants with the baggy seat.

"I *need* help," I said.

Mom had finally shut the refrigerator. But now she was looking out the window over the sink. We live on the second floor of a three-family apartment building. It's a tall, narrow house. Mr. Linaberry, our landlord, lives downstairs from us, which makes Mom constantly worry that we'll be too noisy and disturb him. The Falansons live upstairs. There are only two of them, but when they're home it sounds like a herd of galloping horses trampling over our heads. They never seem to worry about being too noisy and disturbing us.

Where we live now is nothing like the house we had until the divorce. Mom and Dad's bedroom was bigger than our living room here. Mom doesn't even have a bedroom now. She sleeps in the living room, on the convertible couch. Our real house was better in every way. Everything was better then. Even the street name and number were better! 215 Oak Street, on the east side of the city. Now we live downtown at 9½ Degler Avenue. *9½? Degler?*

Last month, on the twelfth, was two years my parents have been divorced. It's not exactly a joyous anniversary. I'd be just as happy if I didn't remember the date. After Dad moved out, he called and came to see us a lot. Then he and Marcia moved to Chicago. They're both lawyers. "Your father has a new life," Mom told us. Right. After that, for all we saw of him, he might as well have been at the North Pole and named Robert Edwin Peary instead of Maxwell Boots.

After my half sister, Rachel, was born, I was curious if she was like me or Wilma. Or completely different. When Dad sent pictures, you couldn't tell. She was just a baby and sort of

10

blobby. We were supposed to visit them a couple times, but it never worked out. Things kept coming up, like Dad having extra work and the baby getting sick.

I glanced at the clock. "If I don't have an opening line, I can't write this!"

"Line . . . ?" my mother said. Finally!

"Yes! For my essay."

"You want me to, ah — "

"Yes! It's due tomorrow morning."

"You shouldn't put things off to the last moment." Mom leaned over my shoulder. "And the topic is — ?"

"A Wish, a Dream." That was the only thing on my paper so far, besides Mr. Pelter's name and room number.

" 'A wish, a dream,' " Mom repeated. "Well, when I was going to school, what I did was take the title and go with it . . . and you know it worked, so . . ." Her voice dropped away. "It's . . ." She nodded. "Yes. Useful method."

Bunny claims my mother has never, ever finished a whole sentence in her life. Slight exaggeration, but you do have to know how to read between the lines. Usually, I don't have any trouble. "You did *what* with the title?" I tapped my ballpoint on the table.

Mom took a pile of dishes and stepped over Chris to the sink. "How about spaghetti and . . ." She ran water over the dishes.

11

Spaghetti and . . . probably meant spaghetti and meatballs for supper. Though it could be spaghetti and butter. Or spaghetti and garlic. I tried to think about my essay, but how could I with the TV blasting and Chris mumbling to himself and Mom crashing dishes around in the sink?

"Mom, what was your suggestion for my essay?" She was looking out the window again, pinching her upper lip. What was so fascinating out the window? I stepped over Chris and looked out the window, too. All I saw was the scrawny little backyard, Mr. Linaberry's red pickup truck, the shed where he had his welding business, and Mr. Linaberry himself, raking up leaves.

"Don't you miss our real house?" I said to Mom.

"Sometimes."

In the yard below, Mr. Linaberry was cleaning matted leaves off the rake prongs. I didn't know much about him, except that he was an awful grouch and a widower and had one son who lived in Denver, Colorado. I also knew he was very neat and clean. Right after we first moved in, Mom had sent me down to his apartment once or twice to ask things, like where the fuse box was. That's when I'd seen his apartment, neat neat neat and dark dark dark. It looked like nobody lived there. It was full of old furniture with wooden arms and claw feet.

I didn't see how Mom could even stand to look out the window at him. He was so ugly, short, with a potbelly and a balding head. And he never smiled, never. Not once in almost two years had I seen him smile, and whenever Bunny came over, no matter how many times I politely introduced her, he didn't say Hello or Glad to meet you, or anything like that. He just barked, "Hello, you!"

I sat down again. "Mom, you were telling me something for my essay, and you never finished." I started out sounding reasonable. Then I yelled, "Mom!" I was in such a bad mood, and I had to do *something* to get her attention.

She turned. "Emily?" she said, as if she'd just realized I was in the room.

"My essay, Mom. My essay!"

"Oh, yes. Well, what I would do is try to incorporate the title in the opening paragraph. Start right off with . . ."

"You mean start with wishes and dreams?" I stared at my paper. I was still blank.

The phone rang. "I'll get it, nobody take it, it's for me," Wilma called. She came running into the kitchen. "It's Max," she said. "I called him this morning."

"You called your father?" Mom said. "When did you do that?"

"When you were taking a shower this morning. I talked to whatsherface. I told her Max should call me."

"Marcia's her name," I said.

The phone rang again. "Oh, I just know it's Max," Wilma said. "Oh, please, I'm praying that it's Max."

"Wilma," my mother said. "Wilma, the phone bill! You can't just go calling long distance. How long did you talk?"

"I'll pay for it," Wilma said.

"With what?" I said. "Your nickel collection?"

My sister picked up the phone. "Boots residence. Dad?" She caught herself. "Max?" Then she held out the phone to me. "It's for you."

"Who is it?"

"One guess," she said disgustedly.

I put the receiver to my ear. "Hi, Bunny."

"What are you doing?" Bunny asked. "I'm trying to write that essay. It's due tomorrow morning. It's driving me crazy! You have to help me, Emily."

"I haven't written my own yet."

"Oh, you'll just dash it off. I know you. Come over here and we'll work on them together. Eat supper with us. My father will drive you home later. Just think, Emily, Shad can make eyes at you at the table! He'll be in little boys' heaven." She's always saying Shad has a crush on me. Even though he's only nine and still in elementary school, it makes me somewhat self-conscious around him.

Mom drove me over to the Larrabees'. I didn't look when we passed our old house on Oak Street.

Bunny met me at the door and threw her arms around me. "Wait until you hear my new joke. A dog went into a pizza place, sat down at the counter, and ordered a large pizza with everything. He ate it all. 'Excellent,' he said, when he was done. The cook said, 'You're a pretty unusual dog.' 'Why?' the dog said. 'Well,' the cook said, 'the other dog that comes in here only orders a slice.' "

I laughed.

"Thank you! I told my father this joke, and he didn't even curl his lip. How am I supposed to hone my comedy skills if he won't laugh at my jokes? Let's go upstairs."

"Did you finish *Great Bones*?"

"I stayed up last night reading it."

"I told you it was good."

"Ma, Emily's here, we're going to work on our essays until supper," Bunny yelled. "You've got to inspire me," she said.

I told her what Mom had suggested about the title and the first line. "But I still don't have my opening," I said. "If I had that, I know I could write the rest." Just as I said it, I thought of it.

The perfect first line. It would lead me right through the entire essay. *The deepest wish of my life is also a dream.*

I sat down at Bunny's desk and started writing. "The deepest wish of my life is also a dream. It's for my parents to be together again, for us to be a family the way we were once. Only it isn't just a dream, it's an impossible dream."

Chapter 3

I was in the lunch line, waiting to buy a carton of milk, when someone behind me said, "If you were the North Star and twinkled, I'd follow you, so I wouldn't get lost."

I looked around.

A boy in a green T-shirt smiled at me. "Hi!" He was big, with brown eyes, tall and sturdy. Big all over — big arms, big legs, a big head.

I picked up a piece of cheesecake wrapped in foil and a container of milk.

"Uh-oh," he said, behind me, "do you know what that cheesecake has in it? Everything but cheese. All chemicals and junk and stuff. Nothing natural."

"How do you know that?"

"I read it in a magazine last night. I saw it on the news. It was in the headlines this morning. Can I eat with you?" he said. "Where's your table? Are you going to sit by the window?"

Who was he? I didn't even think he was in our grade. He looked younger, even though he was so big. Probably a seventh-grader. Was that the way seventh-graders acted? It seemed like a million years since I'd been in seventh grade.

I took my tray across the room to where Bunny was waiting. She was munching on an apple. "The best way to lose weight is to chew each bite of food twenty-five times," she said. "They say it's healthful, but I think it's because by the time you get done chewing, your jaws are so tired they don't even want any more food."

I unwrapped my sandwich and offered her half.

"This apple is plenty for me." She chewed and chewed. "That cheesecake looks really great!" She bent over and sniffed. I could tell she was suffering. She loves cheesecake, too.

The boy with the green T-shirt came up to our table and sat down. "Hi again," he said. "Okay if I sit here? I'm Robertson Reo. You can call me Robby. Or Reo."

Bunny glanced at me with her eyebrows raised. "Bunny Larrabee," she said.

"Bunny Larrabee? That name sounds familiar!" Robertson Reo snapped his fingers in an

18

excited way. "Did I read about you in the paper? That's right, isn't it? Let me think, let me think! Basketball! Right? Am I right? I have a great memory. Something about basketball! Tell me!"

Bunny shrugged. "Sometimes they write me up. I'm a guard on The Lady Chargers."

"Pleased to meet you!" Robertson Reo stood up and shook her hand across the table. "Bunny Larrabee! You're a celebrity. I'm Robertson Reo," he said again. He looked at me. "I forgot your name."

"This is Emily," Bunny said.

Robertson Reo laughed. "I know. I was just kidding. I wanted to see if she believed me. Emily Boots, right? Emily Beth Boots, am I right?"

I drank my milk. I didn't get it. How did he know my middle name?

"Emily, what a super name," he said.

"She's named for Emily Dickinson," Bunny said.

"Who?"

"The poet. Her mom likes poetry," Bunny explained.

He looked at me. "Does that mean you like poetry, too, Emily? Who is this Emily poet? Is she a friend of your mom's?"

"Emily Dickinson. She's dead," Bunny said.

"Was she pretty?"

"What does that mean?" Bunny said. "Do you

19

think every female has to be pretty?"

"Hey, hey, why not?"

"Because it's stupid and sexist."

I frowned at Robertson Reo.

"Oh, Emily, don't give me that look," he said. He was talking and stuffing in food at the same time. "You hurt me with that look. So do you like poetry?"

"Sometimes. Not necessarily."

"*Sometimes! Not necessarily!* That's mysterious. She's being cagey, isn't she, Bunny? She thinks I'm obnoxious."

Did he expect me to deny it?

"I know some poetry I could recite for you, Emily. I know a lot of stuff. I'm retentive. How about the way I remembered about Bunny being in the newspaper? That's the way my brain works. It's like a vacuum cleaner, it scoops up all this stuff and stores it away. Do you know this poem? 'Day is done, gone the sun, uh, da da da, uh something something something.' "

Bunny took another bite of her apple. "Your vacuum cleaner is breaking down."

"It's in there in my brain somewhere. It'll pop out after a while."

"It's not a poem," I said. "It's a song." The summer Bunny and I went to Brownie camp together, we sang that at the end of every day around the campfire.

"Right. A song. I knew that."

He was totally impossible.

"Emily, if you like poetry, that settles it, I like poetry, too. 'Emily had a little lamb, its fleece was white as snow, and everywhere that Emily went, the little lamb was sure to go.' Baaaaaaaa!" he bleated.

Some lamb. He had big ears, I noticed, to go with his big head and his big mouth.

"Emily, I might as well tell you right up front, I'm younger than you, but that doesn't have to matter. How old are you, anyway?"

"Fourteen." I'd had my birthday last month.

"I'm thirteen — almost."

"When?"

"May."

"That's next year. You're twelve," I said.

"It doesn't bother me being the younger man, Emily."

"That's very mature of you," Bunny said. "Isn't that mature, Emily? Aren't you over-whelmed with Robertson Reo's maturity?" Every time she said *mature*, she crossed her eyes.

Robertson kept right on eating, taking huge bites of his food. "Whose homeroom are you in?" he asked Bunny.

"Mr. Clarence's."

"I'm in Mrs. Saginaw's room. What an old fart. She ought to retire and give the world a break."

"I like her," I said. "She's smart and she cares about kids."

"Uh-oh. I guess that means I'll have to like her."

"Just because I like her, *you* have to like her?"

"Right. Whatever you like, Emily, is sacred to me. I'll just have to change my attitude toward Mrs. Saginaw." He crammed in a last bite, gulped down his soda, and stood up. "Don't go away, Emily, I'll be right back." He loped off toward the serving table.

Bunny and I looked at each other. "Who *is* he?" I said. "*What* is he?"

"I think what he is, is in love," Bunny said.

"Yeah, with himself."

"No, with you."

"Oh, no, don't say it."

"Emily, he shows all the signs. He's got Emily fever."

"Oh, no!" I said again.

Chapter 4

Dear Mrs. Watjoichkas,
Bunny told me that Sunday is your birthday.
I think that it is a great thing to live to be old
(excuse me, I hope you don't find that offensive!)
and still have a strong interest in life, which I
know you do from hearing about you from Bunny
and your interest in the Toronto Blue Jays. She
says you are their Number One fan and the great-
est grandmother in the world! Someone who bats
.900. Or maybe it's 1000! Well, Happy Birthday!
And I hope you don't mind getting birthday greet-
ings from someone who is practically a stranger
to you. (I'm Bunny's best friend, and I know how
much Bunny loves you.)
When you were visiting Bunny last spring

23

(well, not exactly visiting, you were recuperating from a stroke), I came over one day to see you. We had a nice talk about Toronto, which I've never been to, and you said I should come and visit there. Well, some day I might! Anyway, Happy Birthday again, and I hope the Blue Jays do great next spring. (To be totally truthful, I don't follow baseball much, although Bunny tells me it's a great game.)

Love to you,
Emily Boots

Dear Mr. (or is it Ms.?) G. R. Immerman,

I just had to write and tell you how much I loved your book Great Bones. I love to read, I read all the time, and I give all the books I love the best to my girlfriend to read, too. Great Bones was one of the best books I've ever read, and since I must have read a thousand books, you can tell that is a true compliment.

I'm quite interested in writing. Would you write back and give me any hints to make me a better writer? Do you think it's weird that I can't write my essays for school until I figure out the first line in my head? I'm so nervous until I get that first line that I just can't believe I'll even write anything good! Then, once I think of that line, I can think of everything else, and I just sit down and write it. My girlfriend thinks this is definitely weird. She has to make an outline. I

*really hate outlines. Do you think that's terrible?
My teacher says outlines are a tool of organiza-
tion. I guess I understand that, but I get all the
ideas in my head, and I don't seem to need the
outline to help me along.*

*Well, enough about me! I hope I didn't bore
you. I'd like to know how long you've been writing, when you got your start, and if you knew
when you were my age that you were going to be
a famous writer someday? Do you have any children? Are you married? What's your favorite
hobby? Mine is reading and writing in my journal! I'll be looking forward to hearing from you
and all your interesting answers.*

*Yours truly,
Emily Beth Boots*

From Emily's Journal

A story I've been telling myself for a long
time. STD. (Since The Divorce). In this story,
Dad calls me and says, "Emily, I've got to
get something off my chest!" And then he
tells me that breaking up with Mom was a
huge mistake. He misses us, his real family.

Both of us, Dad and I, sort of break down
and cry. Then he asks me if we will take
him back. And we cry some more. Then we
call Wilma and Chris and tell them. And
everyone is crying.

Dear Dad,

Well, how are you? I'm quite well. I haven't had a single cold all fall. It's been a long time since I've heard from you, nearly two months since your last phone call. I hope you are okay. I hope you are very okay. Are you still running and keeping in shape?

I'm going to be on the honor roll. I got an A in an essay I did for Language Arts called "Wishes and Dreams." Isn't that a neat title? I love writing things. Mom said she used to write poems when she was in school. But you probably know that. Is it true Mom picked my name, you picked Wilma's, and both of you picked Chris's? I think that's pretty fair. (How about my baby sister's name? Did you or Marcia pick Rachel?) I might want to be a writer someday, Dad. What do you honestly think of that? Mom thinks it's not practical. My other choice is to be a lawyer, like you. I could help people in trouble, I could be a lawyer for poor people, a Public Defender. Or maybe, if things work out, you and I could have a father-daughter law firm.

Well, write me if you get the chance. I sure would like to hear from you! You can count on that.

Your loving daughter,

Emily

P.S. Give my sister Rachel a kiss for me.

Chapter 5

Wilma was making a mask out of a grocery bag. She'd cut out the eyes and nose holes, and now she was drawing a face on it. "Do you like it, Emily?" She put the bag over her head. "It's for art class tomorrow."

I glanced up from the hamburger patties I was making. "It looks good."

"No, it doesn't. I don't even have eyebrows yet." She took it off. "Don't just say everything is okay when it isn't."

I slapped a hamburger between my palms. "Ask Chris next time."

"He never has good opinions."

"I do, too." Chris was reading on the floor,

lying on his back, with his paperweight on his stomach.

"I love doing this," Wilma said, drawing in thick red eyebrows. "I hope nobody knows who I am. I could be a spy with this on, spy on everybody. I love spying on people. It's so exciting. I spied on you once."

"Wilma!"

"I did."

"She did," Chris said from the floor.

"I don't like that." I started frying the hamburgers.

"I didn't see anything. Just you crying."

"It's none of your business if I cry or not."

"Okay, okay." Wilma held up her hands. "We won't talk about it anymore. If you don't want me to be a spy, maybe I'll be a detective. You don't have to go to college for either one. College is a lot of money."

"I'll help you out with money," Chris said. "I'll get a job and give you the money and you can go to college."

"What are you doing when I'm in college?" Wilma asked.

"He's working," I said. "To put you through."

"What kind of job?" Wilma said.

"I don't know," Chris said. "Something good. I want to be rich and buy Mommy a house again."

"Work in a bank," Wilma said. "Mr. Linaberry

said that's where all the money is."

I flipped over the hamburgers. "Why did Mr. Linaberry say that?"

Wilma tried on the paper bag again. Now she had red eyebrows and a bushy red mustache under her nose. "I don't know. We were talking about things."

"What things? You talk to him much?"

"Uh-huh. How is my mask now, Em? Tell the truth."

"It's great."

Wilma looked at herself in the little mirror on the back door. "Yeah, it is great. I could definitely be a spy in this." She tipped her head one way, then another. Suddenly she screamed.

I dropped the spatula and rushed over to her. "Wilma, what's the matter? Did you hurt yourself?"

She screamed again, louder.

"Honey, what is it? Tell me where it hurts." She still had the paper bag over her head. "Take that thing off! Tell Em where it hurts, sweetie!"

She took the bag mask off her head. She was smiling. "I was just thinking, maybe I could be a famous screamer, and I was practicing. People scream on the radio and TV all the time. I bet they have special people to do that, like stunt men. I was reading about them in our school paper."

"Famous screamers?" Chris said with interest.

29

"No. Stunt men. Famous screamers is my own idea. I was practicing to see if I was any good."

"You're not good," I said, "you're great."

She threw her arms around my waist. "You mean it, Em? I could be a great famous screamer?"

"Guaranteed. Good thing Mom wasn't here."

"I would never scream in front of Mom," Wilma said. "She's too nervous."

"Wilma, set the table. Everything's ready. Chris, get the hamburger rolls and the ketchup."

"Let me finish this page, then I will," he said.

"Remember what Mom said? Remember who's in charge?"

"Emily, please, just one more page."

"Chris, with you it's always one more page. Up, boy!"

"Don't talk to him like he's a dog," Wilma said.

Just then, there was a knock at the back door. Chris jumped right up to open the door. He loves company.

"Hello, you kids." It was Mr. Linaberry.

My heart started racing. Why was he here? Had we done something wrong? Maybe he'd smelled the smoke from the hamburgers all the way downstairs. Then I remembered Wilma's scream. I was sure he was going to tell us we were too noisy and had to move out.

"Where is it?" he said. His bald head shone

in the light from the ceiling. He looked over my shoulder.

I wet my lips. "Where is what?" I'd just thought of something else. Had Mom had enough money to pay the rent? A couple of times she'd been short at the end of the month and had to borrow from the bank. I knew this month she'd had a huge bill for the car from Don's Service Station.

"The leaky faucet. Your mama told me, a leaky faucet in the house."

"Oh." I could feel air rushing back into my lungs. Now I saw the toolbox in his hand.

"It's in the bathroom," Wilma said. "Want me to show you?"

"I know where the bathroom is." He waved his hand at her and stumped off through the kitchen and down the hall.

I cut up tomatoes and served the hamburgers. "Sit down," I said. My heart was still sort of thumping around. All the time we were eating, I was aware of Mr. Linaberry in the bathroom. I just hoped he didn't look in the tub! The kids were supposed to wash it after they took their baths, but they always left a greasy ring.

Just when I was clearing away the plates, he started yelling. "Hello. Hey in there! You got a plastic bucket?"

"Tell him just a minute, Wilma." I got the one under the sink and sent Chris with it. I looked at my watch. I was glad it was almost time for my mother to come home.

I was dishing out the Jell-O when Mr. Linaberry came back to the kitchen. "All done," he said. "It's fixed."

"Oh. Good. Thank you."

He stared at me, frowning. Was I supposed to pay him? I didn't think so. It was his house. But I wasn't certain.

"When's your mama coming home?" He blinked and twisted his head around like he had a stiff neck. His eyes were little and bright blue under pale lashes.

"Pretty soon," I said. I sat down and motioned the kids to wait until he left to start eating their dessert.

"What time?" He kept glancing into the corners of the kitchen, like he was checking to see if we were keeping it clean enough.

"In about twenty minutes."

"Uh-huh. Okay." He put down his toolbox with a thump. "She said she had some other things. A torn screen."

"Oh, that's nothing," I said quickly. It was in my room. I didn't want him there. I didn't want him looking at my things. "It doesn't matter, Mr. Linaberry."

"What do you mean, it doesn't matter? Never say that. She says it doesn't matter," he grumbled to a wall. "It always matters. Little thing like a torn screen, you get in bugs, dirt, and then you complain."

"I wouldn't complain."

"Where's the screen?"

"In Emily's room," Wilma said. "Want me to show you?"

"Wilma! You stay here. I'll do it." I stood up and my chair crashed to the floor. It sounded like a bomb going off. At least Mr. Linaberry was up here, not downstairs.

At my room, I opened the door and pointed to the window.

"I need the light, little girl," he said.

Little girl! I flipped on the switch and snatched up some underwear I'd forgotten to throw into the laundry.

"Go back to supper," he said. It was an order. It really made me mad, but I left.

He was only in my room a few minutes, then he came into the kitchen again. "Okay for now," he said. "In the spring, I'll replace it. So where's the mama? She's late tonight?"

"No." He didn't leave. He just stood there. Finally I thought I got it. "Would you like something to eat?"

"A glass of water."

I brought him a glass of ice water. He drank it slowly, staring at the clock over the refrigerator and then every once in a while glancing at the kids.

33

"Would you like to sit down?" I said.

"Okay." He sat down. Chris watched him. I could see the wheels turning in Chris's head. I was afraid he was going to come out with something. But suddenly Mr. Linaberry put his hands behind his ears and wriggled them, as if Chris were a baby he was amusing. Chris smiled politely.

"So what grade in school?" Mr. Linaberry said to Wilma's shoulder. He just couldn't seem to look at anyone straight on.

"Me? Fourth grade," Wilma said. They'd skipped her last year.

Mr. Linaberry tapped his fingers on the table. Wasn't he ever going to leave? Now he was really making me nervous. I went to my room to check that everything was okay.

Wilma followed me a moment later. "I think Mr. Linaberry wants another glass of water."

"Then give it to him! Did he ask for it?"

"No. But he's looking at his empty glass."

"Wilma, we can afford a glass of water."

"I know that! Aren't you coming into the kitchen?"

"I'll be right there." I sat down on my bed. I just didn't like having him in the house. I put on my glasses. I don't know why. Maybe I thought they made me look older and firmer.

Wilma went away, and then Chris appeared.

"Emily," he whispered, "you have to come back. Mr. Linaberry is company. You're not supposed to leave company alone."

"You can keep him company, Chris."

"He's too shy to talk to me, Emily. You have to come."

I went back with Chris. Mr. Linaberry was slowly sipping his second glass of water. I tried to think of something to say. I pushed my glasses up on my nose. Now I was sorry I was wearing them. I could see practically every pore in his skin. "Did you get the yard all raked up?" I asked finally.

"Not yet."

"Oh. I bet there are a lot of leaves."

"Still falling," he said.

At last I heard Mom coming up the stairs. Mr. Linaberry heard her, too. He put down the glass and brushed his hand over his bald head. He sat up straight. His face brightened. It almost started glowing.

I stared at him. Oh, no, I thought. Mr. Linaberry has a crush on my mother!

But there was worse to come.

When Mom walked in and saw Mr. Linaberry in our kitchen, her face lit up, too. Lit up like a neon sign. I couldn't believe it. Later, I asked myself if I had imagined it. I thought I must have. Maybe Mom's face got that bright color because she was embarrassed to have the land-lord in our messy house. But, then, what about that big smile she'd given him? A really big smile! Mom could be sort of absentminded some-times, but she wasn't a hypocrite. She'd acted glad to see Mr. Linaberry. Very glad.

Chapter 6

Robertson Reo fell into step with me as I left school. "Emily! Hel-lo. Can I carry your books for you?"

"No, thanks," I said.

"I happen to be going your way," he said.

"Which way is that?"

"Whichever way you go."

"Robertson, I think I'd like to be alone."

"Why?"

"I have things to think about."

"What kind of things?"

"Sort of personal," I said. I wanted to think about Mom and Mr. Linaberry.

Every single day this week when Mom came home from work, Mr. Linaberry had come up

37

the stairs with her. The excuse was he was helping her with her packages. But he must have been waiting for her! And each time, Mom had made coffee for him and put out slices of cake. One night she'd even broken out the frozen chocolate cream pie we'd been saving for a special occasion. As if all that weren't enough, last night she had gone on a talking jag.

She'd told Mr. Linaberry about the sick kids on her ward and where she went to high school and college, and how much she loved our old house on Oak Street and how sad she was to leave it, but how she wouldn't go back, anyway, for any amount of money, because she hadn't been that happy there. I'd never heard her talk so much.

Mr. Linaberry had sipped his coffee and stared at Mom from those pale blue eyes of his. He kept his eyes right on her, not on the wall, not on her shoulder, but directly on Mom, as if he were afraid to miss a single word.

Later, after I was through with my homework and I'd showered and I was in bed, I could still hear them talking. I used to love to fall asleep to the sound of Mom and Dad talking in the kitchen. Now, I lay awake, trying to convince myself that Mr. Linaberry's coming up to see Mom so much really didn't mean anything.

Probably she was just being tactful and smart being so friendly to Mr. Linaberry. She was protecting our family. He was our landlord, which meant he was almost like a boss over our lives. If we did things wrong in his house, he could kick us out. We could end up homeless on the streets, like people you read about in the newspaper and never think will be you. I shuddered.

"You cold?" Robertson said. Sir Walter Raleigh Robertson Reo started to take off his sweater.

"No, no . . . I'm going straight home, Robertson. I really don't need company."

"Maybe you don't need company, but the question is do you *want* company?"

"It means the same thing, doesn't it?"

He pondered this for a moment. "Right," he said. "Got it. So, is it okay if I walk a few blocks with you, anyway?"

"I really don't feel like talking."

"That's okay. You don't have to say a word. I talk enough for both of us," he said. "I had my fortune told yesterday, Emily Beth. Are you thinking Gypsies, crystal balls, mysterious lights? Forget all that. It was a computerized character analysis. You might ask why I did it, since I know it's not *scientific* science. It's semi-science, or maybe it's only quasi-science. What do you think?"

"I — " I opened my mouth. That was as far as I got.

"Why did I do it? Simple. Out of curiosity. I'm an extemely curious person. I like to be open

39

to all possibilities. My curiosity is the reason I know you, Emily Beth. I saw you in the halls, and I was curious. I thought, Who is that really great-looking girl, and can I get to be a friend of hers? And look! I am! So I figure my curiosity pays off."

In a way, listening to him talk and knowing I didn't have to respond was very restful. I didn't even really mind that he kept me from thinking about Mr. Linaberry and Mom, because when I thought about them, all I did was worry.

"So here's the way this computerized character analysis works, Emily. They took my handprint on a computer and ran it through a machine. It's the old reading-the-palm story, updated. The results?" He gripped my arm for a moment. "I'm going to be completely truthful about this and tell you my weak points as well as my strong points. I'm not going to cover up. The worst result was jealousy. A serious character flaw. Which means to me that if you get interested in another boy, it's going to upset me a lot."

"What?" I said, breaking my silence. I could hardly believe my ears.

"I know I have nothing to worry about right now. You don't have a boyfriend."

"How do you know that?"

"I'm an Emily watcher. And the only person I see you with much is Bunny Larrabee. So, I

40

conclude, no boyfriend. The only thing I want to ask you is if you do get interested in someone, be sure and give me advance notice, so I have time to get used to the idea."

Give him *advance notice*? What was I, a road show? "Robertson, who do you think you are in my life, anyway? I mean, what do you think is your position?"

"I don't actually know," he said. "But I'm hoping. You know. I'm more or less applying for the position of boyfriend myself." He turned his big soft brown eyes on me.

I steeled myself not to feel like a murderer. "You have to stop hoping, Robertson. You're very nice, but you're only twelve."

"What's age got to do with it, Emily? Character is what counts."

"Tell me more about your character analysis. Talk. Let's change the subject."

"Even though I'm on the jealous side, I'm above average in not having a suspicious character. Plus, I have superior sex appeal."

"Wonderful what machines know these days."

"Emily Beth, it was reading just what was written there to be read in my palm print. You want to hear more? I'm above average in speaking my mind. Plus, the analysis went off the chart when it came to me being romantic, loving, and happy about the opposite sex." He beamed

41

at me. "Pretty accurate so far, wouldn't you say? But it did have a few flaws. It said I enjoyed ordering people around. No, I don't! It said I was generous and thoughtful. I hope so. What do you think?"

"About what?"

"What it said."

"Ask your mother. She'll tell you better than I can."

"It also said I was an attention seeker."

"Nooo!"

"Ahh, you think I am."

"No comment. What did this amazing character revelation cost?"

"A mere ten dollars."

"Is it fun throwing ten dollars away? Is it just like tearing it up or setting fire to it?"

"Emily, I earn the money and I spend it. Want to hear the rest? My star sign is Taurus, I was born on a Wednesday, Queen Elizabeth and William Shakespeare are two famous people of my sign. Someday they'll say Queen Elizabeth, William Shakespeare, and Robertson Reo. My birthstone is emerald and my worst fault is being obstinate and stubborn. Plus, my lucky numbers are thirty-five, forty-five, forty-one, fifty-four, and forty-four. Do you get the significance of that?"

"No."

"It's symbolic of your name. Emily. Beth.

Boots. Five, four, and five letters. Five, four, five adds up to fourteen. My lucky numbers all have fives and fours in them, except forty-one, and when you turn that around, it's *fourteen*."

Being in Robertson Reo's company was slightly dazing. I could feel my brain going numb. I was starting to wonder — was it possible those numbers really did mean something?

Chapter 7

Mr. Linaberry came around the corner of the house with a grocery bag in his arms. "Hello, you."

"Hello, Mr. Linaberry." I unlocked the porch door that led upstairs to our apartment. He followed me up the stairs. "Did you want something?" I said, over my shoulder. I tried not to sound anxious. He'd never done this before! I searched my mind for anything the kids had done lately.

"The mama mentioned she needed some things," he mumbled and, in the kitchen, he put the grocery bag down on the table. "Some groceries and things."

Now he was doing our grocery shopping? I

was so stunned, I didn't even say thank you. "How much do we owe you?"

"Nothing now."

I took out my wallet. I had twelve dollars. I held it out. "Is this enough?"

"Not now. Not now." He flapped his hands, like pushing me away. "I'll settle with the mama later."

Every time he said *the mama*, my skin jumped. At least he didn't hang around. When it was time to feed the kids supper, the bag was still on the table. I didn't even want to touch it.

"Where'd all this stuff come from?" Chris said, peering in. I told him. "Mr. Linaberry gave this to us? Wow!"

"He didn't give it to us, Chris, he just bought it for Mom. People don't *give* us things." I glanced at the clock. Mom usually got home from work around seven. Was she going to come in alone or with Mr. Linaberry?

"We launched a helium balloon at school today," Wilma said. "It was a special day, wasn't it, Chris?"

"Yeah," Chris said. He had a bicycle painted on his cheek. Wilma had a heart on hers.

"Do you want to know why we launched a helium balloon, Emily?" Wilma said. "It was for books. We've been reading all month, and we put a big card on it with everybody's name and favorite book and a note to whoever finds the balloon to send the card back to us. Are you listening, Emily?"

"Uh-huh."

"Miss Perry says last year her class got the card back from Houston, Texas."

"My teacher said once he got a card — " Chris began.

"I'm telling this, Chris," Wilma said. "You eat, then you can talk. I wrote on my part of the card, 'Wilma Boots. *The Trouble with Thirteen*, by Betty Miles.' Did you ever read it, Emily?"

"Uh-huh."

"Did you like it?"

"Wilma, I'm the one who told you it was a great book."

"You did not. I found it myself. I found it in the library, and it's my favorite book."

"Uh-huh."

"Why do you keep saying uh-huh? Uh-huh is boring!"

I took my dish to the sink. "I'm trying to think, Wilma."

"What are you thinking about?"

"Nothing . . ."

"Nothing means you don't want to tell me."

The breakfast dishes had been soaking all day. I pulled the plug and watched the greasy water gurgle down the drain. I wished I could wash away my thoughts as easily. I didn't like Mr. Linaberry, and I didn't like this *Mr. Linaberry*

46

thing with Mom. But what could I do about it? Put frogs in his bed? Sure, Emily. How about putting on a sheet and haunting his house? Fab. Are there more stupid thoughts where those came from?

Maybe I could call my father and discuss it with him. That wasn't juvenile, but it was just as ridiculous as the frog and ghost thoughts. Should I talk to Mom? But what could I say— that I didn't like her choice of friends? Maybe the best thing would be to go to the source, right to Mr. Linaberry, and tell him to stay away from Mom. Great. And have him get mad at us and put us out on the street.

I sprinkled cleanser all around and scrubbed the sink. Around and around I scrubbed. Just like my thoughts about Mr. Linaberry and Mom . . . around and around . . . and around . . .

I thought I had made it clear to Chris about the groceries, but the moment Mom walked in, he greeted her with, "Mom! Mr. Linaberry gave us a whole bag of stuff. Wait 'til you see."

"Chris, what did I tell you?" I yelled. "We're going to *pay* Mr. Linaberry. Tell him, Mom."

Mom started taking out the groceries. "Oh, wonderful." She stacked cans of salmon in the cupboard. "What a help this . . . Emily? Is everything . . ."

"Everything's fine. The kids ate their supper. I put the mail on the TV. The electric bill came.

Nobody called. Mr. Linaberry brought the groceries up." I stared at her. "Why did you ask
him to do that? I could have done the shopping
for you."

"You do so much already, Em," Mom said,
"and he has the truck. Such a sturdy little truck,"
she said in a fond voice, as if anything of Mr.
Linaberry's was wonderful. It was too much for
me.

"Mom!" I drew in a breath and plunged in.
"I don't want to be mean about this, but I honestly don't get what you see in Mr. — "

"We had macaroni for supper again," Wilma
complained, interrupting me. "Will you tell Emily not to make macaroni all the time, Mom? This
is important! I want to have other things. I'll
throw up if I have to have macaroni again."

"For someone who hates macaroni, you
scarfed it down," I said.

"Shut up, Emily. Butt out of my private talk
to Mom."

Mom put away the last of the groceries. "Isn't
Mr. Linaberry good to do this? I mentioned that
I needed . . . but I never thought he'd . . ."

Wilma went around the side of the table and
knocked into me. "Me Tarzan, you monkey
puke."

"Very mature," I said. "Mom, I want to talk
to you — "

48

"Please, girls," Mom said. "Don't start . . . I just got home . . . and all day it's been . . ." She sighed and took Wilma into her arms for a kiss. "Emily . . . Wilma . . . keep the peace, okay?"

"What did I say?" I was suddenly really upset that Mom hadn't even noticed when I tried to have a serious talk with her. And now she was putting Wilma and me in the same breath, as if we were the same age.

"Well, I should go down and pay Mr. Linaberry," Mom said.

"I'll do it," I said. "How much is it?"

Mom touched me on the shoulder. "Thank you, darling." But then she went out the back door and downstairs herself.

I got my books and sat down at the kitchen table and tried to study. Bunny phoned, and we talked for a while. When I hung up, I looked at the clock. Mom's routine — I mean, before Mr. Linaberry started showing up in her life — had always been to take a shower as soon as she got home from work. After that she'd get into her old flannel robe and soak her feet in a pan of hot water while she read the newspaper and drank a cup of tea. Then she'd have supper. She always said doing things that way made her feel human again after working in the hospital all day.

Well, how did she feel now? Like a monkey? She was still downstairs. No shower yet. No foot soak. No cup of tea. No supper. I looked at the clock once more. She'd been gone over an hour. How long did it take to hand over a few dollars?

Chapter 8

"Bunny? Hi, it's Emily. Guess what? I heard from the guy who wrote *Great Bones*. He didn't answer any of my questions. He acted offended that I'd asked. He just about said, Butt out of my personal business, kid!"

"Oh!"

"Do you think it's an imposter writing the letter? The book was so good, I thought G. R. Immerman would be really nice. How could a nasty person write a nice book?"

"Was the letter really that mean?"

"Wait a sec, I'll read it to you. Ready?"

"Go."

" 'Dear Emily, There are some rules for writing, I suppose, but most of them aren't very helpful. My own rule is to know what I want to say, say it, and get the hell out. I don't like bad actors who hang around smirking at the audience, waiting for the applause. Since I'm not a teacher, this may all be a crock and you can forget it. As for my personal life, that's my business, not yours. Read my books. That's all you need to know about me. G. R. Immerman.' "

"It wasn't really *mean*, Em. It was more like he's somebody's grouchy uncle. He probably doesn't mean to sound so brusque."

"Maybe you're right. But I'm disappointed. When I read his letter the first time, I decided I'm never going to read his books again!"

"Em, that's dumb!"

"Bunny, I came to that conclusion myself. I was just going to tell you. Give me a chance to finish what I'm saying."

"So sorry, Miss So Sensitive."

"Bunny, that's not very nice!"

"Well, you are."

"I'm *what*?"

"Sensitive."

"Bun-ny!"

"Em-ily!"

"Good-bye, Bunny. I don't want to talk to you anymore right now."

"Talk to you tomorrow, then."

"Maybe."

"Ha! You will. You will, you will! If you don't talk to me, Emily, I'll talk to you. Don't hang up yet, Emily! You forgot to say good-bye to me."

"Good-bye, Bunny!"

"Hel-lo! Who is this?"

"Excuse me, who do you want?"

"Hel-lo! Is this Emily? Emily Beth Boots? Hel-lo! Can you guess who's calling you?"

"I think I have a pretty good idea. Could this be Robertson Reo?"

"The one and only. But remember, you can call me Robbie. Or Rob, if you like that better. Or Reo. That's my favorite. Emily Beth — "

"You know, Robertson, my name is Emily. Nobody calls me Emily Beth."

"Just me?"

"Yes."

"Great! I'm never going to stop calling you Emily Beth. It's my special name for you. Well, Emily Beth, you want to know the point of this phone call? To hear your voice!"

"Okay, you've heard it. So we can hang up."

"I like your sense of humor. It's dry and witty. You say what you have to say. A woman of few words. I like that. Emily Beth, I got the idea to call you when I was reading something that reminded me of you. . . . Aren't you going to ask me what I was reading?"

"I know you're going to tell me whether I ask or not."

"Emily Beth, you're probably the prettiest girl I ever saw."

"Where'd you read that, on the front page of the newspaper?"

"Ha! ha! ha! No, here's what I read, and it was on page eight of the newspaper, third column over, in case you want to check it out. Eight hundred and forty-six songs were recorded last year in this country with the word *love* in the title."

"That's . . . very interesting."

"Eight hundred and forty-six. It makes you think, doesn't it?"

"What does it make you think?"

"It makes me think that when I write a song I definitely won't put love in the title, because I don't want to be like everyone else."

"I don't think you ever have to worry about being like everyone else, Robertson. That is one thing you definitely don't have to worry about."

"Well, thank you, Emily Beth. I consider that a compliment. And I would say this has been an excellent conversation. On a scale of one to ten — "

"You'd rate it a ten?"

"Absolutely. Wouldn't you?"

"I don't think I'd be that rash."

"Ha! Ha! Ha!"

"Look, I have to go now. I have things to do. Good-bye, Robertson."

"Good-bye, Emily Beth. When I write that song I'm going to put your name in the title."

"Hello?"

"Emily, this is Dad."

"Dad? Dad! Where are you?"

"Chicago. How are you, Emily?"

"I'm fine, Dad. I'm just so surprised! I didn't expect it to be you. When the phone rang, I thought it would be one of my friends, Bunny or — "

"I'm sorry you didn't think it would be me. I guess you have no reason to think it's going to be me when the phone rings. I haven't been the best about calling."

"Oh, no, Dad. It's not that — "

"No, no, I know, I've been remiss. Are you mad at me?"

"No, Dad!"

"Honey, I honestly think about you a lot. And I mean to call, I really do. Practically every day I think about it, and then something always happens."

"I know. I understand."

"Life is pretty hectic here, things come up all the time. The job is a lot of work. A lot of building going on. Every building has its contracts. Paperwork, paper, paper. The whole thing has me hopping, a lot of pressure, a lot of deadlines. I should have an assistant, but I'm not going to get it. Money's too tight."

"Do you have to pay for an assistant?"

"No, no, honey, I work for the city. They have to pay, but they won't. You know how that is. . . . Tell me, how are you? Did I ask you that already? Emily, Chicago's a great city. Big, big city. Very different experience from living in a small town. I wish you were here, honey. You'd get the big-city outlook. It would be good for you."

"Dad, there was something I wanted to ask you — "

"So you're doing top-notch work in school, aren't you? I got your letter. I'm glad you wrote. Very glad. I know I should write, too, but it's like the phone calls — I have the intention, and then something always gets in the way."

"That's okay, Dad. I know."

"And I feel bad that I missed your birthday. I'm going to make it up to you. I've sent you some money, and I want you to spend it on nice things for yourself."

"Thank you, Dad!"

"It's not that much. I hope you can get something nice with it."

"Dad, I was going to say — "

"Listen, sweetheart, Marcia wants to say hi to you."

"Hello, Emily? This is Marcia. Your daddy and I were so happy to get your letter. He's just so overwhelmed these days with work. I guess I don't have to tell you. You know how he is, how hard he works. He just throws himself heart and soul into his job. Well, 'bye, Emily, it was great talking to you. Here's your dad again, Emily, eager to talk to you."

"Hello, honey. So were you telling me everything's okay back there with you kids? Wilma and Chris are doing all right? They're doing good in school?"

"Yes. You know how smart they are. Dad, there is just one thing — "

"I want to talk to the twins in a few minutes, honey. Time's running out and I'm going to have to hang up."

"It won't take long, it's about Mom — "

"Your mother? How is she? She's still working at the hospital, isn't she?"

"Yes. She's at work right now."

"You tell her I called you, okay?"

"I will."

"Don't forget, sweetheart."

"I won't."

"Because she's after me to pay more attention, and I want her to know that I called. I mean, she's right! I don't deny that, but I want her to know — "

"I'll tell her you called, Dad. I won't forget."

"I know I can count on you. Maybe you should let me talk to Chris and Wilma now."

"Sure, Dad, but what I wanted to say was — well you see, our landlord, Mr. Linaberry, lives downstairs, and Mom is always worrying about making him upset with noise or things like that. Well, but now he's been coming up — "

"Sweetie, is this going to take a while?"

"Well, I just thought I'd explain the background — "

"Maybe you should write me about it. Or we can talk the next time I call. But let's say goodbye now, sweetheart, and put on the twins."

"Okay. 'Bye, Dad."

Chapter 9

After I talked to my father, I was so mad at myself. I didn't say one thing I meant to say to him. I just kept saying Yes Daddy Yes Daddy, as if everything were perfect. Why did I do that? Even when he asked me if I was mad at him, I quickly said, Oh, no! But that's not true. I am mad at him. I mean, I don't *just* feel mad, I feel other ways, too, but sometimes I wake up in the middle of the night, and I feel so mad I cry. Why didn't I tell him that? Instead I said *Oh, everything's fine, Daddy!* Am I a coward or what?

Last year, Bunny got me to do something I'd never done before — scream at my father. Maybe that doesn't sound so great; you're supposed to respect your parents. Bunny's point is this: They should respect you, too, but how can they if they don't know what you're thinking or feeling? I'd been really upset about something my father did. To tell the truth, I don't even remember the details now, except that it had something to do with plans for visiting, which were going all wrong. I was falling all to pieces over it, and Bunny finally said, "Emily! Call him up and tell him straight out how you feel."

I thought, Oh, no! I can't do that! That's what I always think. I didn't want to hurt his feelings. I didn't want to upset him. But then, I did it. I got up my nerve and I called him. I don't remember anything I said, but I do remember that I sort of screamed at him, which isn't like me at all. I don't like to scream at people. I don't like to get mad at people. I don't like to cry in front of people. I think emotions are private, and you should keep them private.

Bunny is so different. Maybe her way is better than mine. She definitely seems like a much happier person most of the time. I get these depressions — like after the phone call with my father — and I think of all the things I did wrong and said wrong. And I wish that I could do things better and differently.

My father's present to me came in the mail the next day, and on Saturday, Bunny's mother drove her to my house, and we took the bus to the mall. It was a perfect day. Blue sky and a good fall smell of leaves in the air, and Mom was home and I didn't have to think about Chris and Wilma. And besides all that, I had money in my pocket. "I feel great!" I told Bunny when we got to the bus.

"Me, too!"

"You always feel great."

"Not always."

"Bunny, you're always cheerful and full of jokes."

"I have a serious side," she said.

Then two high school girls sat down in front of us and we shut up. The blonde one was going through her pocketbook. She threw everything out and started moaning. "I forgot my hairbrush, Jamie! Oh god, I forgot my hairbrush, did you bring a hairbrush? Oh god, Jamie, this is a disaster!"

"Don't tell me, Kim. I have my own problems," Jamie said. "I'm wearing my shirt out."

"So?" Kim said.

"So, like, I don't like it that way," Jamie said.

"Well, like, tuck it in," Kim said.

"Well, I don't like it that way, either. That's the problem. So tell me what to do."

Bunny jabbed me so many times, I was sore afterwards. As soon as we got off the bus, she did a perfect imitation of Jamie and Kim. "My hairbrush! My day is ruined! I forgot my hair-brush and my shirt is out. My life is in a shambles!''

I started laughing and couldn't stop. From then on, everything struck me funny. When we stopped to eat at a new place, I thought it was hilarious that it was called Space Out and every-thing on the menu had names like Quark Salad or Comet Soda. The servers were wearing caps with green antennae and the name tag on the girl who took our order said ASTRA. Maybe it struck me funnier than it did Bunny. After all, her sister's name is Starship. (Bunny says her mother was in a cosmic phase when Star was born.)

While we were eating our Spaceburgers (really, your basic cheeseburger on a round roll), we both watched a man across from us who was plugged into a cassette player, eating, reading the newspaper, and filing his nails, all at once.

That was the kind of day it was. A great day. Even perfect. Then I got home and found Mom's note, and I got that flat feeling, like air going out of a balloon. Her note said Wilma was at Sally's house, Chris had gone to a Little League game, and there was pea soup in the fridge for supper. Then there was a P.S. That was the needle that deflated the balloon. ''P.S. Gone for a drive with Mr. Linaberry.''

All I could think about after that was Mom and Mr. Linaberry driving around in his pickup truck and — *what?* What did people their age do when they went out for a drive? Make out? No way could I imagine my mother doing that! But then, why did she go for a drive with him? For the pleasure of his company? What was she thinking of?

After Wilma came home, she and I walked over to the park to pick up Chris. Then we made supper. Chris gave us a moment-by-moment account of the game, and I kept Wilma from going berserk over the pea soup, which she hates, by letting her add chopped-up hot dogs, which she loves.

After supper we did the dishes, made popcorn, and turned on the TV. Still no Mom. I did some homework, then I went into the kitchen and phoned Bunny. "What are you doing?"

"Playing Scrabble with my mother, and she's beating me. She's too smart for me. What are you doing?"

"Nothing." I glanced at the clock again. "Did you see Robertson in school yesterday, following me around?"

" 'Emily had a little lamb . . . and everywhere that Emily went, that lamb was sure to go.' Remember? It's love, Em."

"Why couldn't someone handsome and sixteen fall in love with me? Bunny, what do you think a ticket to Chicago costs? I want to save up to visit my father."

"I don't know. Four hundred dollars? Five hundred?"

"I'll never be able to save that much!"

"Make a deal with your mother. You save half and she gives you the other half. That's what my parents do."

"Mom would just say she doesn't have half."

"How about your father?"

"I don't want to ask him. I just want to make the money and buy a ticket and go out there and say, Hi! I thought I'd drop in on you . . ."

"What a great idea, Emily!"

"You like it? I just thought of it this minute. I wish I hadn't spent the money he sent me."

"But it was fun, wasn't it?"

"I'll have to get a job. What kind of work do you think I could get?"

"Baby-sitting?"

"When can I do it? I always have to take care of Wilma and Chris."

"You don't have to take care of me *ever*," Wilma yelled. She has ears in the back of her head.

Bunny and I talked about an hour. Mom still wasn't home.

I made Wilma and Chris take their baths and get into pajamas. I fixed them cocoa with marshmallows and I let them watch some more TV. And Mom *still* wasn't home! Just when I was thinking I should start calling the police and the hospitals to see if there'd been an accident, in came Mom, smiling and cheerful, in her fuzzy pink pants and matching pink top.

"Where were you?" I said.

"Out for a drive, sweetheart. Didn't you see my note?"

"Yes, but look at the time!"

"Well, it is a little late . . . but — "

"A *little* late, Mom! It's almost ten o'clock. What time did you go out?"

"What time did I . . . around five, I suppose."

"Five o'clock is when I came home. You were gone already."

Mom sat down on the couch and took off her shoes and unclipped her earrings. Pink shells to match her outfit. "Emmy," she said, "I work every day. I work when I get home. I don't go out, do I? Well, today I just felt like — " She waved her hand in the air. " — fun," she said.

"Fun?" I said. "With Mr. *Linaberry?*"

She looked at me a long time. Then she said, "Yes. Fun with Mr. Linaberry. I've gotten to really appreciate him. He's a shy man, Emily."

"Mom? Mr. Linaberry, after *Dad?* I don't get it."

"Your father doesn't come into this. Did you ever think I might be lonely? I'm surprised at you, Emily. You don't consider me."

I flushed. "Mom, I just don't see what you see in Mr. Linaberry."

"You don't know the real person."

I felt like saying, *And I don't want to know him!* "What'd you do?" I said finally.

Mom blinked. "Not that much. We drove around . . . out to the lake, and we watched the sunset. And then we ate supper, fish and ice cream. And we . . . laughed."

I'd never even seen Mr. Linaberry smile. "What did you laugh at?"

"Things," Mom said.

I didn't say anything else. What else was there to say?

Chapter 10

Each of the three apartments in our building has a tiny front porch. As I came home from school, I saw that on the top porch, the Falansons had a line of washing strung out. His and hers jeans and underpants. On our porch, I could see the top of a tent Chris and Wilma had rigged with sheets and boxes. On Mr. Linaberry's porch, a rake and shovel stood in the corner, and Robertson Reo sat on the front steps.

"Hel-lo, Emily Beth."

"What are you doing here?" I said.

"I came to see you. Don't you want to say hello to me?" He was wearing a blue T-shirt and khaki shorts that showed his long thick legs, which were sprawled out as if he owned the spot.

"How did you know where I live?"

"A little birdie told me."

"Aren't you supposed to be working?" I said. "I thought you had a job."

"I do. I deliver newspapers in the morning. Did you ever do that?"

I shook my head. "I wouldn't mind, though. I need to earn some money. I was thinking of putting an ad in the paper, but it's kind of hard for me to find time to work."

"Do you want to know what I was thinking about, sitting here waiting for you? I've decided to go into politics when I grow up, and run for governor of the state."

"Why not President, while you're making plans?" I walked around him and took out my key.

"Where are you going? You can't go yet. You have a visitor. I came all the way over here to see you."

"Well, we've visited." I unlocked the door.

"Emily Beth! You can be harsh."

Maybe he didn't mean anything by it, but that upset me. I'd been feeling sort of weepy and tense all day. I was probably going to get my period. "Robertson," I said. "I don't think I'm harsh. I'm just doing what I usually do when I come home, which is go into my house and take care of my sister and brother."

"Don't you like me at all?" His eyes had that puppy dog look.

"I don't know if I like you or don't like you. All I know is, you've been following me. In school, Robertson Reo. On the street, Robertson Reo. And now — here you are again!"

"I like you, so I like to be wherever you are. And I keep hoping you'll look at me and like me, too. Do you think that's romantic? My mother says people have to get to know each other to really love each other."

"Your mother's right."

"Well, remember the character analysis said I was romantic."

I stuck my head in the door and yelled up the stairs. "Wilma! Chris! Are you guys home?"

"They're here," Robertson said. He looked at his watch. "They got home about thirteen minutes ago."

"How do you know my sister and brother?"

"I introduced myself. That's how you get to know people. I was sitting here on my uncle's porch, waiting for you, and these two kids come along and the girl says, Who are you? So I — "

"Wait a second. Back up. Did I hear you say you were sitting on your *uncle's* porch?"

"Right."

"That's what I thought I heard," I said. "Are you telling me Mr. Linaberry is your uncle."

Robertson nodded. "He's my mom's older brother."

"Good grief," I said. I felt like fainting. Was it a plot or something? Robertson and his uncle out to get me and Mom? I knew that was crazy, but I couldn't help thinking it. Then I wondered if Robertson had said anything to his uncle about me. My face flushed hot. I hated people talking about me!

"Are you going to stay out here and talk to me for a while?" Robertson asked.

"No."

"Why not?"

"I told you I have stuff to do. Why do you keep asking me things like that? Why are you such a pest?"

He stood up and sort of hung his head. "Is that all you think about me? That I'm a pest?"

I stood there, half in and half out of the door. That was the way I felt about Robertson liking me — half in and half out. Even if he was young, he was cute, and I have to admit it was flattering to have him like me so much. But it was also sort of annoying the way he constantly dogged me. It was just something else I didn't need in my life at the moment.

I took the mail out of the box and went upstairs. About ten minutes later, I went out on the porch and looked down. Robertson was still there. "What are you doing?" I said. "Aren't you going home?"

"I'm waiting to see my uncle."

"He's probably out back in his welding shop."

Robertson snapped his fingers like I'd given him the most brilliant suggestion in the world. "You're right again! Thanks, Emily Beth!" He got up and went around the side of the house.

Chapter 11

"I need to see a picture ID to open an account," the woman behind the desk said. She was a tall African-American woman, wearing glasses. "Sit down, dear. You, too," she said to Bunny.

I dug into my purse and came up with my laminated school photo, the one we use on the cafeteria line and for games and dances.

"This is you?" she said, looking at me, then at the card. "Are you sure?"

Bunny looked over my shoulder. "That's Emily. I can vouch for it, I'm her best friend."

"You don't think it looks like me?" I said.

The woman smiled. "No, I don't! Unless you're thirty-five and your own mother." She

72

got up. "Hang on, I'll be right back." She went off to another area of the bank.

"I didn't think it was that bad a picture," I said to Bunny. "I wasn't even wearing my glasses in it."

"What gets me is that it's so hard to open a savings account! Wouldn't you think they'd just take your money and say thank you, and that would be it?"

I nodded and counted my money again. Thirty dollars, and I'd earned it all in less than a week. Four hours cleaning out a cellar and two hours mowing grass. If I could do that every week, in three months I'd have enough for a plane ticket to Chicago. The only thing I didn't like about it was that the money came from Mr. Linaberry.

Last week he'd come upstairs and asked if I wanted to work for him. "I own two other houses," he said. "I could use the help now and then."

"Well, I have to take care of the kids," I said.

"Your own time," he said. "Whenever."

I looked at Mom. She nodded her head that it was okay. Later I realized it couldn't be a total coincidence that I'd mentioned to Robertson that I wanted to earn money and then his uncle offered me work. Did Robertson think that was going to make me like him more? That seemed a little sick. But I liked working. Mr. Linaberry wanted the cellar cleaned out. Sunday afternoon I carried boxloads of junk out of the cellar and loaded them into Mr. Linaberry's pickup truck. It was kind of neat seeing the cellar empty out. And the pay was really good, more than I could ever make baby-sitting.

"What's Mr. Linaberry like as a boss?" Bunny asked.

I shrugged. "Okay." I couldn't say anything bad about him, but that didn't mean I wanted to say anything good, either.

"Are you going to work for him again?"

"He said if he thinks of anything else I can do, he'll call on me."

"Oh, so it isn't regular."

"I wish it was."

We sat in silence for a minute, then Bunny said, "You know what I just thought? Emily, if your mother got serious about Mr. Lina-berry — "

"What do you mean, serious?"

"Serious, like married him. If she — "

"Married him! Are you crazy, Bunny?"

"If she did, though, that would make Robert-son your cousin."

"Bunny, my mother's not going to marry Mr. Linaberry. It's a stupid idea. Don't even say it!"

"Well, I bet if I'd asked you a month ago if you thought your mother even *liked* him, you would have laughed in my face. And now they're very very buddy buddy, right?"

"Buddy buddy? They're not kids at camp."

"You know what I mean. Friendly. Maybe even friendlier than friendly."

"What does that mean?"

"Sex?" Bunny said.

"Shut up, Bunny! They're too old for that."

"My mother says people are never too old."

"You talk to your mother about stuff like that?"

"Sure."

I just looked at her. Sometimes I envied Bunny her family. When my parents were splitting, I used to pretend I was going to live with the Larrabees, be their third daughter, because I knew they would never split up. But other times, like now, I knew that I could never fit into that family.

The bank rep finally came back. She had papers for me to sign. Then she took my thirty dollars and went away again. When she came back, she gave me a stamped receipt and a black bankbook with a gold seal. "There you are. Good luck, dear."

As soon as we were outside, I opened the bankbook and looked at my name and the neat little notation of my first deposit. "Next time I come, I'll have earned interest on this," I said.

"Right. In a month, you'll have made at least fifteen cents," Bunny said.

"Well, it's still fifteen cents more than I'd have if I didn't put it in the bank."

We hung around the mall a while. We were in the bookstore, browsing, when I heard someone say, "Hel-lo!" I didn't even have to turn around to know who it was. "Find something good to read?" Robertson said.

"Hi, Robertson," I said. "You know Bunny."

"Bunny Larrabee," he said with enthusiasm. "The great basketball star. The female Jabar." He did a pantomime of a skyhook and gave her his 500-watt smile. We stood around talking for a few minutes, then Robertson said, "You girls want to go get something to eat? My treat."

"You're paying? You don't know how much Bunny eats," I said.

"Thanks, sweetie," Bunny said.

"Order anything," Robertson said, when we were standing at the counter. He took a wad of bills out of his pocket. "That's all you're going to have, Emily Beth?" I'd ordered a soda.

"Bunny'll make up for me," I said.

Bunny kicked my leg.

Obviously I wasn't in my most tactful mood, and when we sat down with our trays, I blurted to Robertson, "Where did you get so much money?"

"My friend is so subtle," Bunny said.

"My paper route is a little money machine," Robertson said. "I built up the route. I make customers and I keep them. I'm one of the best. It's a good way for anyone to make money. You don't have to work that hard, but you do have to be consistent. You have to get up early every morning."

"Don't you have to be strong to carry the papers?" Bunny said. "The Sunday papers must weigh a ton."

"That's a special route," Robertson said. "There's a guy with a station wagon who does that. I have a carrier I put on my bike for the daily papers. Some people use shoulder pouches, but that's brutal."

"I'd like a paper route," I said. "Regular work, regular pay. Sounds good."

"There's a long waiting list," he said. "I know one girl who had to wait six months for her route."

"Oh. I need money lots sooner than that."

Robertson leaned his big head toward me. "You could share my route. We could do it together. Go out every morning, you take one side of the street, I'll take the other. Fridays, we collect. We'll split the profits."

"Why would you do that for me?" I asked.

"Why wouldn't I? I like you." He stuck out his hand. "What do you say, want to be partners?"

I didn't know what to say! It would mean seeing Robertson every single day. I looked at Bunny for a sign.

"Go for it," she said, pouring ketchup on her fries. "What can you lose?"

"Sleep," my mother said. "That's what you can lose, sleep. You're still growing. You need your sleep."

"Mom, I need to make money!" We were sitting on my bed, facing each other, knee to knee.

"Emily . . . listen to me. I'm a nurse, I know what I'm . . . And you can't afford to lose it at your age."

"Lose what?"

"Sleep. What are we talking about?"

"I thought we were talking about money! I told you, *I need money!*"

"What is the big . . . I really don't understand," she said softly. "All of a sudden, you want want want." She'd brought her knitting in, and now she opened the bag and took out the needles. A long, shapeless gray something dangled from them.

"I don't just *want want want*. It's for a reason. I'm saving so I can visit Dad in Chicago."

She looked up. "Oh." Her hair was in her face. Messy. She'd put on lipstick after her shower, but she'd smeared it. She'd put on her old frayed robe. Suddenly I hated the way she looked so much I couldn't sit there one more second.

I scrambled off the bed. "Mom, this is a good opportunity. There aren't that many ways kids my age can make money." I went to the window and turned my back so I wouldn't have to see her. "You didn't mind when I cleaned the cellar for Mr. — " I was so mad I couldn't even think of his name! "A plane ticket is expensive. I have to earn a lot of money."

"Your father should buy the ticket for you." She was knitting so fast her needles hit each other.

"I want to buy my own ticket."

"What about baby-sitting?" she said. "You can always . . ."

"Sure, on Saturday nights, *if* you're not working. Once a week, that's how much you'll let me baby-sit. I'll be old and dead before I save enough money that way!" In the other room I could hear the TV and, over that, Wilma's voice going on about something.

"Anyway, next week you start working nights again," I said. "Did you forget? That means I have to be here every single minute after school and every evening. The only time I can work is in the morning. A morning paper route is perfect! Please, Mom, say yes!"

"Sweetie, I would, but your health is more

important than money." She got up and bent to kiss me.

I felt like jerking my head away. I didn't. I just stood there like a statue. I didn't kiss her back.

Chapter 12

". . . and this man was wearing a mask," Wilma said in a deep voice, "because he was going to kidnap this kid and drag him to where he lived with the lady in this dirty spidery place under a porch."

Chris's mouth was open. He stood in the middle of the kitchen, twisting the napkins in his hand. "So what happened?" he quavered. Two more words out of Wilma and tonight he'd have living-color nightmares.

"Wilma, you're talking too much," I said. "Are we going to have this party or not?" I smeared more strawberry icing on the cake.

"The man and woman lived under a porch?" Chris said.

Wilma nodded and dropped a stack of silver on the table. "They were crazy and dirty people, and they got kids and tied them up. You better watch out for them."

I glanced at Chris. "Wilma, let's get this party on the road."

The birthday party for Mom had been Wilma's idea. I was just going along. I was still mad at Mom for not letting me take the paper route. I'd made the cake, true, but the kids had done practically everything else — picked out the recipe, planned the menu, and decorated the house with balloons and streamers.

"Do you want to know what the man and woman did to the kids, Chris?" Wilma said.

"Nothing," I said. "They didn't do anything. People don't live under porches and kidnap kids." I put the frosting bowl in the sink and ran hot water.

"You're wrong, Emily. It's a true story," Wilma said.

"Wilma, give it a rest."

"What do you know about it?" she argued. "Lyda Storch told me in school, and her father's the sheriff, and it's a true story."

"Well, I don't want to hear any more about it. And I mean it," I snapped.

Wilma and Chris finished the table. Next to Mom's place, they put the evening newspaper folded to the back page, where all the birthday greetings were printed. Right at the top of the page in a box were the words, "Look for ANN BOOTS at Community General Hospital tomorrow. Then be sure to wish her a fabulous 38th birthday and oodles of love from her kids — Wilma, Chris, and Emily." Below that was a picture of Mom from when *she* was a kid. She had cheeks and ponytails and ribbons. The greeting had been Wilma's idea, too.

"Mom is going to be so surprised," Wilma said with satisfaction. She stood back with her hands on her hips.

"I'm hungry," Chris said.

"You can't eat," Wilma said. "We have to wait for Mom today."

They were both watching the clock. When we finally heard Mom on the stairs, they raced to the door. "Happy birthday, Mom! Surprise!"

"Oh, what is this?" she said. She looked all around. "It's beautiful, beautiful . . ." Right away, she wanted to give me credit for it. "Emily!"

"Don't look at me." I gave her a cool smile over the kids' heads.

"Me! I thought of everything, Mom," Wilma said. "I made all the decisions. I picked out the recipe for the cake."

"Mom, the balloons were my idea," Chris said.

Mom kept going ooh aah, this is so great, so

beautiful. I leaned against the wall with my arms folded. Mom complimented everything. When she saw the newspaper with the birthday greetings, she got teary. "I'm so proud . . . You're all so sweet!"

I brought the casserole and biscuits to the table. I didn't say much. Still, everything was okay until the cake. Then Mom said, "We should invite Len . . . to share!"

"Who?" I said. But I knew.

Mom sent Chris downstairs to get Mr. Linaberry. When he came in, he didn't really come in. He just stood by the door in that hunched odd way of his. His blue eyes darted around from one of us to the other.

Mom went and took his hand. "Come and sit down, Len. Look at this party my children made for me. Look at this cake!" He sat down, and she cut him a slice of cake.

"Hello. Hello." Mr. Linaberry bobbed his head to us.

I stared at him in sort of horrible fascination. How could my mother like him? How could she take his hand and touch him? I couldn't understand it. He was ugly and strange. Maybe he was even stupid. I tried to feel sorry for Mom. She was lonely. No, it was worse than that. She was desperate, and it was making *her* act stupid.

I wished I would never have to see him again in my life. I hated the thought that he put his

paws on Mom. Had he kissed her? Ugh! I fell
back in my chair, staring at the cake. And then
I started getting bizarre thoughts like Mr. Linaberry's wife coming back, so he would lose interest in Mom. Coming back from where, the
dead?

I poked at the cake, pushing it around on the
plate. Everyone else was eating and laughing
and talking. Why was I so upset? Mr. Linaberry
wasn't anything to me. Less than nothing! But
sometimes a person who's less than nothing to
you becomes important in your life, whether you
want them to or not. Like Marcia. She hadn't
been anything to me, either, until she became
my stepmother. What was the difference if Dad
chose a Marcia and Mom chose a Mr. Linaberry?
Was she choosing him? My heart just seemed to
fall away inside me.

I got up and went to my room. "Where're you
going, sweetie?" Mom said. She sounded so
happy. I closed my door, but I could still hear
everyone talking. "Mom's birthday greeting cost
us fifteen dollars!" That was Wilma. Next she'd
be telling everyone I'd taken the money for it
out of my bank account. I heard Mom laughing,
I heard Chris talking, I even heard Mr. Linaberry
finally saying something.

Mom called me again. "Emily? You coming
back?"

"Maybe." But I stayed in my room, reading

and trying not to think of how Mom had taken his hand and brought him to the table; how she had said, Oh, we have to invite Len to share this with us.

Len. And did he call her *Annie?*

I read the same page over and over, not making any sense out of it, and I started to cry.

Chapter 13

The weather turned warm at the end of October.
Everybody said it was Indian summer. Mr.
Cooper, the gym teacher, took our class outside
to play softball. I was doing okay. I made two
base hits and caught one fly ball, then I saw
Robertson sitting in the bleachers. And I lost it.
I'm not the world's greatest athlete, even under
the best of circumstances, and it flustered me to
have him watching. After that, I didn't do anything good in the game.

Later, when I complained about it, Bunny just
laughed. She thinks I exaggerate everything,
anyway.

"I did so bad in the last three innings," I said.

"I know I'm just average in sports, but I want to be better! I hate that I did so bad."

"Em, you're an outstanding writer. You can't be outstanding in everything. Look how doofy I am about writing. You're too hard on yourself. You want everything and everyone to be perfect."

Did I? I'd never thought of it that way. Were my expectations too high? Wasn't it right to want to be the best and want other people to be the best, too?

That evening, Mom came into my room. "I want to talk to you," she said, and she sat down on the edge of my bed. I closed my book. Mom didn't say anything, just started brushing her teeth in an absent way. She was in her pj's. Finally, I said, "Mom, did you come in here to brush your teeth?"

She looked at her toothbrush as if she didn't even realize she had it with her. "Oh! Well, what I came to say is I think you have a wrong . . ."

I waited. "A wrong — "

"Idea."

"About what?"

". . . Len . . ." she said after a moment.

"I don't have any idea about him," I said quickly.

"Well, yes you do. And it's wrong. He's a very nice man. Quiet . . . still waters. You've heard,

88

Don't judge a book by its cover. And that's what you're doing, Emily."

I thought of all the stories I'd read about people misjudging other people because of really superficial reasons, like the way they looked or sounded. And then in these stories they always learned that they were dead wrong. The person they'd misjudged turned out to be the one who saved their life or was the smartest or most courageous. Was that Mr. Linaberry? I didn't think so!

"I know you're not an intolerant person," Mom said. "Or impolite."

"I'm polite to him!"

"But not friendly — "

"Mom, you can't force somebody to like somebody they don't like."

"You should be nice to my friends. I'm nice to your friends."

"I know," I muttered.

"So . . . will you?"

"What do you want me to do, Mom? Tell me exactly. Give me orders. I'll follow them."

Mom laced her fingers together. "Well . . ." She gave me a tiny smile. "Let's not talk about that anymore, now. You just think about it." She bobbed her head.

I stared at her. She was doing what Mr. Linaberry did — that same head-bobbing motion!

"Friday, we're going out," she said. "The movies. It'll be a treat."

All of us going to the movies together *was* a treat. "The twins'll be excited," I said.

"No, darling. I mean Len and . . ."

"Mr. Linaberry? You're going out with him?" I was sort of trembling inside. "It's a date?"

Mom nodded. "So, you'll take care of the kids, won't you?"

I started to say Yes, and then words came out of my mouth that I didn't even know were there. "Friday night? Oh, no, I can't, Mom. I've got a date, too."

"You do? Who with?"

"A boy in school."

"What's his name?"

"Nobody you know."

"Could you change it? Friday night is my last free night this month." She was going on evening shift starting Saturday.

"I guess so, but — "

She bobbed her head again. "Oh, well, listen. Have your date. I'll just change mine — or something."

I pulled up the covers. "Okay. If you're sure." I was starting to feel guilty for ruining Mom's date. But then I reminded myself I wasn't doing it to be selfish. I wasn't doing it for me. It was for *Mom!* I loved her, and I didn't want her to be lonely, but Mr. Linaberry wasn't the answer.

She wasn't setting her sights high enough. She deserved someone smarter and nicer, and yes — even if looks *were* superficial — someone better looking, too. Someone the twins and I could look up to and admire and like and be glad he was in Mom's life.

Chapter 14

I was in the kitchen in the morning, fixing lunches and half listening to the radio, when I heard Wilma say to herself, "Open your hand and let the butterfly go slowly."

It sounded so profound that I turned around and just looked at her. "What does that mean?"

"I don't know."

"Where did you hear that?"

"Our teacher told us."

"Oh." For a moment I'd been hopeful that "let the butterfly go slowly" meant something so smart that it would light a candle in my mind and help me out of the hole I'd dug myself into. *Big* deep hole. I'd told Mom I had a date Friday night. And now I had to make it come true. Who was my date? Where was he? How was I going to find him?

There was a riff of music on the radio. Then the announcer's voice. "And now let's have a word with Barb Germander, a champion marathon runner. Barb, what's the best thing about being a runner?"

"Well, frankly, Mark, what I love about the sport is that you're half naked. When I run, it's a little crop top, little shorts, maybe flower print tights — "

"Half naked," Wilma shrieked. "Chris, did you hear that? It was on the radio. Half naked!"

I turned off the radio. It was all static in my head, anyway.

"Don't you think Charlie Dana is perfectly adorable?" Bunny said. "His eyes are just like Nicholas whatshisface, the actor."

"Uh-huh."

We were standing by the corner window on the second floor, looking out over the playing field. That is our favorite place to talk. Bunny says someday, when we're both famous, she as an athlete, me as a writer, the school will put up a plaque right here to our friendship.

Bunny sighed. "Charlie Dana. Isn't that an adorable name? Only I hear he has a temper. Lucy Chen said she knows for a fact that when

Charlie Dana doesn't get his way, he throws a tantrum."

"Really!" I was only half listening. Actually, Charlie Dana had given me a long look in the corridor yesterday. Bunny was right, he had gorgeous eyes. What if *he* asked me out on a date? What if I asked him? I couldn't! I'd never have the nerve. Besides, if Bunny liked him . . .

"What do you think about Marshall Quinn?" Bunny said. "Is he the ugliest boy in the world, or is he not?"

"Oh, Bunny, no. He's kind of cute in a funny way." What if I asked Marshall to be my date?

"Cute? Marshall Quinn? He ought to have plastic surgery, so someone will go for him someday."

"Even if he doesn't," I said, "if he's got two legs and is male, some woman will want him." I heard my voice wobbling.

Bunny put her hand on my arm. "Em, are you getting sick?"

I shook my head miserably. Then I told her about Mom and Friday night, and how I'd said I had a date. "Now what am I going to do, Bunny? I feel so stupid!"

"Em, take it easy. The answer's staring you in the face. Robertson."

"Bunny, I can't go out with him!"

"Why not?"

"He's too young. He didn't ask me. I don't

want to. Are those enough reasons? No? How about this — I've been pushing him away for weeks, and suddenly I'm begging him to go out with me?"

"Not begging, Em, just asking. Uh-oh, speak of the devil, here he comes."

I peered blurrily down the hall.

"Hi, young Robertson," Bunny said.

"Bunny. Emily Beth. How do you girls feel about the difference between taking a shower and taking a bath?"

"Is this a dirty joke?" Bunny said.

"Absolutely not. It's a sober question in the interest of truth. I'm taking a poll for the school paper."

"In that case, I favor showers," Bunny said.

"Would you care to say why?"

"Quicker. Cleaner."

Robertson jotted it down in a little notebook he took out of his shirt pocket. "How about you, Emily Beth?"

I looked at him. My lips moved. Nothing came out.

"Shower or bath?" he said encouragingly. "Let me make that clearer. Emily Beth, do you prefer showers to baths? A simple yes or no will do."

Once again my lips moved. This time, words came out. "Would you go to the movies with me Friday night?"

My fate was sealed.

Chapter 15

"I'm meeting him there, at the movie, Mom," I said.

"He's not picking you up at home?"

"Mom, I told you, I'm meeting him at the mall."

"Well, when I dated . . ."

"I know, Mom, the boy always picked you up at home." I knotted a scarf and tied it around my forehead. "What do you think? How does this look?"

"Everything looks wonderful on you, sweetheart."

"Oh, Mom, that's not true. Wilma, come here and tell me if this looks okay."

Wilma surveyed me from head to toe. "The

scarf is okay. The bracelet is gross."

I took off the bracelet. I was wearing black jeans, a blue printed shirt, and a long knitted sweater that reached my knees. I was ready. Sort of. Before I left, I called Bunny.

"Give me some moral support," I said. "Tell me again why I'm doing this." I spoke with my hand cupped around the phone.

"Because you're a rotten kid who doesn't want her mother to enjoy herself. . . . Why are you still home?"

"I don't want to be too early and just hang around."

"Well, don't miss the bus."

"I can always take the next one, Bunny."

"Then you'd be late."

"Bunny, don't make me more nervous than I am already."

"You're nervous about *Robertson?* Emily, it's just little old, big old Robertson. You sound like you could use a joke to loosen you up. Did you hear the one about the three Martians who — "

"Bunny, no jokes. I'm not in the mood. I'm relaxed," I lied. "I'm going off to meet Robertson with a smile on my lips."

"And a song in your heart?"

"Right."

"Good. Robertson couldn't have put it better himself."

When I got off the bus in front of the theater,

he was waiting for me. "I got the tickets," he called, holding them up.

"How much do I owe you?" I said, opening my purse.

"Nothing."

"Robertson, I have to pay for my ticket."

"No, you don't. I have lots of money."

"I don't care how much money you have. It's not a matter of money. That's a very obnoxious way of talking."

"I just meant that a couple of tickets won't wipe me out."

"I suppose you think it would wipe me out?"

"I didn't say that," he protested.

"Actually, I should be paying for your ticket, too. And I will. I'm the one who invited you." I opened my wallet and took out money.

"You can't pay for my ticket." He shoved his hands into his back pockets. "I'm the boy!"

"Excuse me, what's that got to do with it?"

"Boys pay," he said, as if it were truth engraved in stone.

We stared at each other. I had my hand out with the money, and he had his hands pushed in his back pockets. What was I supposed to do — knock him down, sit on him, and shove the money into his pocket?

Finally, I put away my money, and we went inside. He bought a box of popcorn. I bought the sodas. We were early. The lights were still on in the theater, and we stood at the back, looking down the rows of red seats. "I like to sit up front," he said. "Second row."

"That's too close for me." I pointed at two seats in a middle row. "Those look good."

He followed me, but when I started in, he said, "How about a little closer?"

I went down another row. "Okay?"

"It's still too far back for me."

"Robertson, if you want to sit up front, go ahead. I'll sit here." I sat down. He sat down next to me. "You can go up front," I said. "Honestly, I won't mind."

"No, I'll stay here."

"Are you sure?"

"Emily Beth, I'd rather be with you. I'd rather be with you than anything."

"Oh," my face got hot.

The lights went down and the coming attractions started. I slipped on my glasses. Movies were one place where I really had to wear them. "I love this stuff," Robertson said. "Sometimes it's almost as good as seeing the movie." He stared at me. "I didn't know you wore glasses."

"Do you think they're ugly?"

"No, they're cute. They look cute on you."

"No, they're ugly."

"You're wrong, Emily Beth." He put his arm around me, squeezed me, and whispered, "Men are animals, and I'm no exception."

"Adorable," I said sarcastically, but it was, kind of.

An ad for an airline company appeared on the screen. Then another ad. Then a cartoon telling us to be polite and not talk during the feature. Then a warning against smoking. Finally the movie started.

And just then, two people went down the aisle on our right and sat down a few rows ahead of us. I stared at them disbelievingly. It was dark, but not so dark that I couldn't recognize my own mother. Or the person with her.

Mom and Mr. Linaberry. Here! So, she had her date, after all! Even with all my planning. I took off my glasses and started chewing on the stems. Why would Mom come to the same movie I was at? Had she forgotten? She could be absentminded, but this was too much! And who was watching Wilma and Chris? Had she forgotten them, too? I couldn't believe that. Maybe she'd asked our upstairs neighbors. But, why? They'd never been the least bit friendly to us.

Don't ask me details of the movie. I spent more time watching Mom than anything else. When Mr. Linaberry's arm dropped across the back of Mom's seat, I almost leaped into the air. It was a miracle I didn't shout out loud, *Get your hands off my mother!*

The movie seemed to go on forever. I sat there,

turning hot and cold, seething and freezing, and making up speeches in my head, things I knew I'd never have the nerve or the presence of mind to say. *Mom, you have to believe me — I want you to be happy. I'm not a hard-hearted monster. In fact, no matter how much you irritate me, I happen to love you a lot. I have your best interests at heart, and that's why I'm telling you to drop Mr. Linaberry — right away! Fast! Forever!*

The music swelled. I turned my eyes to the screen again. A beautiful girl was lying in a hospital bed, sobbing quietly. Who was that sitting next to her? Oh, yes, her mother, who was going to be totally devastated when the beautiful girl, her daughter — I'd forgotten her name, although it must have been used two hundred times in the last hour — died. I could tell she was going to die because of the music. Besides, in the movies it was always the beautiful people who died.

Robertson looked at me. "Sad movie," he said in his loud whisper. "How do you like the actress?"

"Wonderful," I whispered back. I reached for the popcorn box. Empty.

"Want me to get some more?" he said.

"No, that's all right."

"You sure? I don't mind."

"Shhh! Shhh!" someone behind us said. Mr.

Linaberry turned around. I sank down in my seat.

The girl died. There was a funeral. The mom sobbed bravely. The scorned young lover lurked in the background. He hadn't been good enough for the beautiful girl, according to her mother. It was like my mother and Mr. Linaberry and me, but in reverse — plus the scorned young lover, unlike Mr. Linaberry, was athletic, handsome, and smiled a lot.

The scene changed. The scorned young lover and the mother met in the street. They talked. He spoke about her daughter from the heart. You could tell that he loved her better than anyone else ever had. . . . Suddenly I realized the movie was just about over, soon the lights would come up, and then Robertson and I would be face to face with Mom and Mr. Linaberry. And then what?

Would nephew and uncle wink at each other? Would Mr. Linaberry be pleased as punch that his nephew was out with Annie's daughter? The two delighted boys who got their wimmin! And would Robertson be overcome with pleasure to meet my mother? I could hear him saying it. *Mrs. Boots, I'm overcome with pleasure to meet Emily Beth's mother!*

On that thought, I was up and out of my seat. Robertson was right behind me.

"Where're you going?" he stage-whispered.

I held my throat. "Fresh air. Gotta have fresh air." That wasn't too much of a lie. I felt nauseous.

Outside, he said, "Are you okay?"

"Much better!" I gulped in air. "I'm sorry I made you miss the end of the movie."

"It doesn't matter. You could tell all they were going to do was walk off into the sunset together, talking about her daughter."

"She was pretty, wasn't she?"

"Not my type. Did you ever notice, Emily Beth, how in movies ugly people never die? I mean if they do, you're glad. They don't die in sad ways. But the pretty people always get knocked off slowly by vicious killer diseases."

I looked at him. I couldn't believe he'd said it. It was exactly what I'd been thinking.

"Uh-oh, look at that," he said. A couple was standing in the doorway of a store with their arms wrapped around each other.

"Don't *stare*," I said. "Don't point! It's private, Robertson."

"But they're right out in public, Emily Beth. They must want me to stare." And he actually stopped so he could stare even more.

I walked away from him. I couldn't figure this kid out. One minute he said something really cute and smart, and the next he acted like a total jerk.

He caught up with me. "What's the matter? Are you mad at me or something?"

"I hate people who are snoopy. I'm sorry to be so blunt about it."

"Well, Emily Beth, they're still right there in public, kissing. Glued together." He glanced at his watch. "They must have been kissing for two minutes already. Want to time them and see how long they go on?"

"No." But then I checked the time, too. And I waited with him. I pretended to be interested in the architecture of the stone house on the corner. What a hypocrite. At least Robertson was up front about his staring.

"Three minutes," he reported. ". . . they're going for five . . . six . . . seven . . ." At eight minutes we agreed they had probably broken all the records, and we moved on.

"Well, that was certainly enjoyable," he said.

"Better than the movie," I said.

At Grove Avenue, which was halfway between his house and mine, we said good-bye. "I had a great time," he said. "I have to thank you for asking me."

"I had a nice time, too," I said.

"My pleasure, Emily Beth!" His eyes shone at me. "I should walk you home."

"No, you don't have to do that."

"I want to do it."

"Robertson, is this going to be like the tickets?"

"Not if you don't argue," he said. And he walked along with me. So then we had to say good-bye again in front of my door. He held my hand and squeezed it. "It was great, it was so great."

"Okay . . . thanks." I squeezed his hand back and ran up the stairs. If only I hadn't seen Mom at the theater, I would have had a really good time.

The evening had been one surprise after another. Liking being with Robertson. Seeing Mom at the movies. And now I had the third surprise. I opened the door, and guess who I found in the living room, watching TV and baby-sitting my sister and brother?

My best friend, Bunny Larrabee.

"Yeah, it's me," she said. "Your mom called about five minutes after you left and asked me what I was doing tonight. I said, Nothing special, just sitting around watching TV."

I moaned.

"Then she said she had a favor to ask me, if I would baby-sit the twins tonight."

I sighed and sat down next to her on the couch.

"What could I do? Tell your mother I didn't want to help her? Or should I have told her that

105

you were trying to keep her from going out? Which was why *you* went out. And that you were going to kill me when you got home and found I'd made it possible for *her* to go out, after all." Bunny drew a breath. "Which one, Emily?"

I slumped down. "All of the above," I said glumly.

Chapter 16

Monday morning I woke up sick and went back to bed. My legs were wobbly and my head ached. "Flu," Mom said. In the middle of the day, the nurse called from Wilma and Chris's school. They were both sick. Mom brought them home and put them to bed, too. "At least you're all sick together," she said, as if that were an accomplishment. Actually, we almost always get sick at the same time. Mom took care of us until she left for work around three o'clock. Same thing the next day and the next. Every day after she left, Chris would start crying, "I'm lonely for Mom."

And every day Wilma would moan, "Shut

up, please shut up, I have a headache."

And then I'd totter into their room and read them a story to distract them. I knew just how Chris felt. It is sort of lonely not having Mom around when you're sick. It's not just that she's a nurse and can take your temperature and stuff (I can do that, myself), but she has these little special things she does that make you feel better. She changes your sticky pillowcase every few hours. If your throat aches, you get soothing things to eat like ice cream and tapioca. If it's your head aching, a warm washcloth. And she always makes sure you have enough tissues and books and games.

But on Thursday, Mom came down sick, too. I'd been sick the longest, so I tried to take care of her, but even something as simple as making her a cup of tea or bringing her another blanket still seemed like a huge effort. "What a crew we are," Mom whispered weakly. She was on the couch. Chris and Wilma had dragged their pillows and blankets into the living room and were lying on the floor near Mom.

I thought I should make supper for everyone, but Mom said it was okay if we just ate toast and ice cream. "You still are weak, Emily. . . . I'll be better tomorrow . . . and I'll make you all good food."

We were finishing our ice cream and watching TV when the phone rang. It was my father.

"Hello, sweetheart," he said. "It's a month! How about that?"

"What about a month, Daddy?" I croaked. My voice was still really weird-sounding.

"I told you I'd call in a month, and here I am."

"Let me speak to Dad." Wilma poked me. "Let me speak to Max."

"Wilma wants to talk to you, Dad."

"Are you okay, Emily? Your voice sounds funny."

"I'm sick. We're all sick with a flu, even Mom. I didn't go to school all week. Mom says it's the worst flu we've ever had."

"We got the same thing," Dad said cheerfully. "First me, then Marcia. Fever and aching bones, right? I stayed home, but Marica went in to work, anyway. You want to say hello to Rachel? She's right here. Say hello to your sister, Rachel!"

There was a little pause, then I heard a squeaky voice saying, "Hi, hi, hi. 'Bye."

After me, the twins talked to Dad and to Rachel. Chris stayed on the phone the longest. "This is your big brother," he said to Rachel. "What'd you do today?" He listened, then he said, "What are you going to do tomorrow?" And he listened again.

After he hung up, Wilma said, "I don't get it. Was she talking to you? All she said to me was Hi."

"That's all she said to me, too," Chris admitted. "But I think she understood everything I said to her."

"You're a crazy bird," Wilma said.

Saturday morning, Mr. Linaberry knocked on our door. "Hello, you," he said, looking over my shoulder at Mom, who was lying on the couch, the same place she'd been for the past two days.

Mom tried to sit up. "Oh, Len. Len."

"I wondered," he said. "I didn't see you."

"Oh . . . well . . ." Mom sort of gestured around at the mess and at herself, then fell back on the couch. "You can see . . ."

Mr. Linaberry nodded. "Uh-huh, uh-huh." He came in and peered into every room, even the bathroom. "Huh! Huh!" he kept saying, like he couldn't believe what he saw. The house *was* pretty messy. The kitchen sink was piled with dishes, and nobody had taken out the garbage for days. Plus there were clothes and papers and odds and ends of things everywhere. He came back into the kitchen, carrying a load of clothes, and he put them into the washing machine. "Where's the soap, little girl?"

I went under the sink for the detergent. Who had given him permission to do our laundry? We could take care of ourselves! I ran hot water into the sink full of dishes. I grabbed the broom

and swept the floor. Meanwhile, Mr. Linaberry
had found a rag and was cleaning the stove.
"You don't have to do that!" I said. I must have
gotten a jolt of adrenaline to my system. I started
racing around the apartment, cleaning like a
maniac. I hadn't moved so much, and definitely
not so speedily, all week. I did the dishes,
stacked books, and folded the newspapers for
recycling, into a paper bag. I even stripped the
twins' beds and made them up fresh. *And* remembered to dump the old sheets into the ham-
per, out of sight of Mr. Linaberry! I didn't stop
cleaning for a moment. Neither did he — he vac-
uumed the living room, washed the windows,
and polished Mom's favorite brass lamp.

"Everything is so . . . *clean!*" Mom sighed,
when he finally left.

Five minutes later, he was back, this time carrying a pot. "Soup," he announced. He went
into the kitchen, poured the soup into cups, and
handed them around to everyone. "Should be
homemade," he said. "I didn't have time."

"Oh, no. This is wonderful," Mom said.

Mr. Linaberry offered me a cup of soup. "No,
thank you." I put some tuna and crackers on a
plate and took it into my room. Maybe the rest
of my family didn't have any pride, but I wanted
our *own* food. I sat on my bed, nibbling a cracker
and taking tiny bites of the tuna.

Mr. Linaberry didn't leave for a long time.

Finally, I went back into the living room and sat down in the rocking chair near Mom. Mr. Linaberry was playing cards with Chris and Wilma. "You. Want to play?" Mr. Linaberry asked, looking at me, or rather, at my shoulder.

I shook my head. What gave him *that* idea? And when was he going? He'd been here for hours. Was he planning to move *in*? "How do you feel, Mom?" I asked.

"Better," Mom said. Her eyes glowed like Chris's had, with fever. Or was it love?

"The mama ate all her soup," Mr. Linaberry said.

"Good!" I said crossly. The traitorous thought had slipped into my mind that my father probably wouldn't have done half of what Mr. Linaberry had for us. We used to joke about how when anyone of us got sick, Dad was so upset, he had to leave the house . . . so he wouldn't see us suffering.

Mom touched my arm. "Emmy . . ." she whispered.

"What?"

"Isn't Len a fine, fine person?"

I didn't say yes. I didn't say no. I rocked harder. Okay, he helped us out. That was a fact. He cleaned, he brought us food. Why? Because he was so good? Or because he wanted to impress Mom? I knew which one I thought was the right answer.

When he finally got up to leave, he shook hands with Chris. "Don't forget me, Len," Wilma said. He shook hands with her, too. He turned to me. I didn't offer my hand, so he gave me a tap on the head. Then he went to the couch, bent over Mom, and kissed her. There was worse to come, though. Mom raised herself up and kissed him back.

Chapter 17

"Emily Beth Boots, hel-lo."

"Robertson Reo, how are you?"

"My health is impeccable. How's yours?"

"I'm coming back to school tomorrow."

"Hey, hey, hey. I await the moment with anticipation."

"Thank you, Robertson."

"Emily Beth, do you like me?"

"Yes."

"I know you do! You've been converted."

"Converted? I wouldn't put it that way. You make it sound like a religious experience."

"I won you over by the power of my personality. I made a stand and it paid off. You don't know this, but I directed powerful beams of en-

ergy thought to you. That's why you asked me
to the movies. I'll tell you the truth, Emily Beth,
I didn't believe it could work. I was a skeptic,
myself. I got this idea of concentrating mental
energy from an article I read in my dentist's
office. I said to myself What do you have to lose,
Reo? Give it a try! I concentrated on you. Every
time I saw you, every time I thought about you,
I sent powerful beams of energy thoughts your
way. Bingo! You asked me to the movies."

"Robertson, take it easy. You don't know the
whole story."

"My uncle says you were pretty sick there for
a while."

"Excuse me? Your *uncle* says. I don't appreciate your uncle talking about my private
affairs."

"He didn't say anything private, Emily Beth,
he just commented."

"I do not appreciate your uncle commenting
about anything about me."

"It wasn't you especially. Your family. Wilma
there and the other one — "

"Christopher."

"Riight. And your mom, Ann — "

"My mother is *Mrs. Boots* to you, Mr. Reo."

"Emily Beth, I think you're mad at me."

"I am not mad at you."

"Excellent! I wouldn't want you to be mad at
me. Hey, hey, hey, guess what? Your mother,

115

I mean *Mrs. Boots*, and my uncle were at the same movie we were at last week. The same time even."

"Imagine that."

"Oh, you knew it!"

"Yes, I did, Robertson."

"It's funny we didn't see them."

"Do you talk to your uncle a lot, Robertson?"

"What's a lot? Give me an example."

"A lot is talking about when he was at the movies and about me being sick. I think that's a lot."

"Emily Beth, my uncle Len's a funny guy. He's kind of an oddball. My aunt died a long time ago, and my mother says ever since, Uncle Len has been a different person. My mom calls him once a week to check up on him, and then she hands me the phone and I have to talk to him. He doesn't say much, so I have to think of things to say, like 'Hi, Uncle Len, I saw a movie the other night with my girlfriend — ' "

"I'm not your girlfriend, Robertson."

"Or maybe I'll say, 'So what did you do today, Uncle Len?' You know, try to get him to talk a little, give me a rest from it."

"What kind of a person was he before your aunt died?"

"More of a regular person. He used to be a fireman. He was even a hero. Mom has newspaper clippings pasted into our photo album when Uncle Len rescued two kids. He rescued other people, too. He inhaled so much smoke, he damaged his lungs and had to leave the force. That's when he started his repair shop. Am I boring you?"

"No. That was interesting. I'm pretty surprised about your uncle being a hero. I'm impressed. He doesn't look the type. Robertson, I have to go now. But I have two things to say to you first. One. I am not your girlfriend. I am a friend who is a girl. And, two. Do not talk to your uncle about me or my mother."

"Why not?"

"Because I say so."

"Got it! Anything my girlfriend wants, she can have."

"Good-bye, Robertson!"

Chapter 18

From the moment I went back to school after I got well again, I had a problem with Robertson. He'd changed. Just because we'd gone to the movies — or, no, maybe because I'd *asked* him to the movies — he thought he had a claim to me. Before, he'd always been bordering on the impossible but somehow kept it in check. Now he'd gone all the way over the edge. He thought I was his, and he wanted the world to know.

It began the day I returned to school. Bunny and I were eating lunch in the cafeteria when Robertson saw me. He was at the other end of the room, but he stood up and bellowed, "Emily

Beth! There you are!" Everybody's head turned. Everybody looked at Robertson, then at me. Robertson sounded as if he'd been searching the world for me for years. "You look great!" he yelled. "You don't look sick at all!"

Then he charged across the room and lifted me off the bench. He was strong, and it happened in an instant. He was laughing, but I wasn't. I felt like a toy, one of those little floppy things whose arms and legs dangle.

Almost every day that week there was another Robertson incident. He'd catch up with me somewhere, in the hall or outside on the steps, and say something like, "Cats purr before they die, Emily Beth. It's a scientific fact." And then, with me off guard, he'd move in, rumple my hair, pat my shoulder, or put his hands around my waist.

I'd say, "Robertson, hands off, please."

And he'd say, "But Emily Beth, I love you."

And I'd say, "Robertson, don't say it. Don't think it. Forget it!"

He'd smile and back off — for the moment. The next day or the next hour, or sometimes in the next minute, he'd be back again, watching for me in the halls, swooping down on me, getting his arms around me. I know it sounds like he was just being affectionate. But it was something else. It was possession. He acted as if I were his, as if he could do anything he wanted, pick me up, put me down, turn me around, rumple my hair, *whatever*, just because he "loved" me.

I got so I dreaded seeing him. What made it really weird was that when he acted normal, I liked him. He could be a very sweet nice guy. One day it was raining and he gave me a ride home on his bike. He acted perfectly. We talked in a friendly way. I thought, Good! That's out of his system!

But the next day, he saw me in the hall and came straight for me, and it started again. The grabbing and squeezing. He gave me a little shove and push, back and away, like I was his favorite rag doll.

"What am I going to do about him, Bunny?" I said, as we were leaving school. "He's getting out of hand."

"You have to tell him, Em. If you don't, you can't expect him to change. You have to set the limits and make it really clear. My father says everybody is entitled to their own space. He says sometimes people don't act right, just because they don't know what the limits are."

Bunny's father is a psychologist, so Bunny knows a lot about these things, too. She's been a help to me lots of times. (One funny thing, though, is that sometimes she and her father have the biggest fights in the world.)

120

"So I'm supposed to just tell Robertson, cool it, or something?"

"Just say what you feel. Tell him how you feel when he grabs you. Give him the word straight, Em."

"What if he doesn't listen?" I said nervously. "You know the way he talks."

"He'll listen," Bunny said. "People are much better at listening than you think."

The next day I tried to do what Bunny said. We were in the cafeteria again. This time, we went up to Robertson and sat down at his table. I put on my glasses, just to make the point that I was dead serious. "I want to talk to you, Robertson."

"Great! I want to talk to you, too! You're going to Picnic Day, aren't you?" He stared at my glasses. "You do look cute in those things! Wear them to Picnic Day."

"Don't be ridiculous."

"I'm happy I'm going to be seeing you at Picnic Day," he went on, as if he didn't see me every single day.

"The whole school goes to Picnic Day," I said. "You'll see *everybody* there." I thought that might get him in the right mood to understand what I wanted to tell him about limits.

"I just want to see *you!*" He rumpled my hair.

I jerked away. "Don't do that!" I almost shouted.

"Robertson," Bunny said quickly, "Emily wants to explain something to you."

"Right," I said.

"About the picnic?"

"No!"

"Robertson, Emily wants to explain how she sees your relationship."

He looked happy. He put down his sandwich. "I'm listening, Emily Beth."

"Robertson — " I cleared my throat. "Now, you know I like you, but there are limits to what — "

"I like you, too." He slid closer to me on the bench.

"Stay right where you are! What I came here to say is, we're friends, and friends don't go around mauling each other."

"Of course not."

"Friends talk to each other."

"We talk a lot," he said happily.

"You're not hearing me. Let me tell you again. We're friends, but that's it. Just *friends*. Which means we respect each other. We don't pummel each other." I looked at Bunny. She nodded encouragingly and mouthed the word *space*. "We give each other space," I said.

"Got it," he said.

But from the look in his big brown eyes and the way he was leaning into me, I knew he hadn't.

Chapter 19

Neither my mother nor I had mentioned Mr. Linaberry for a while. But every once in a while, I'd see signs around our apartment that he'd been there. Like finding the loose tiles in the bathtub replaced. Or the crack in the living room wall fixed. Or the bad burner on the stove turning red hot one morning when I switched it on. I could never forget about him. Even if I didn't see him, he was always there, living right below us or working out back in his welding shop.

Then, one day, when we had a half day so teachers could go to a conference, I came home and found him in our kitchen with Mom. I'd come rushing in, not thinking about anything special, just calling Mom. Then I saw the two of them. They were eating lunch, that's all they were doing, but it felt like something else to me. They were sitting elbow to elbow, and Mom was still in her bathrobe.

I didn't like it. I didn't like Mr. Linaberry being there. I didn't like the pizza on the table. Or the coffee they were drinking. Maybe my face got red. It seemed to be burning. Mr. Linaberry nodded to me. I dropped my books on the counter and went to the refrigerator.

Mom said, "Hello, sweetheart, I forgot . . . half a day. Hungry?"

"No." I was, though. I poured a glass of juice and gulped it down.

"Plenty of pizza. We can't eat all this . . ."

"I don't want any."

Mr. Linaberry stood up. "I'll go now. You can eat. It's okay." He almost smiled at me. My face was burning more than ever.

Mom walked with him into the living room. I heard them talking to each other, murmuring. I imagined they were standing by the door, standing close. Maybe Mom was slumping a little because she was taller then Mr. Linaberry. What were they saying? Were they talking about me? I sat down at the table and sniffed the pizza. It smelled delicious, but I didn't touch it.

Mom came back. She poured another cup of coffee and sat down across from me. "If you want to say something, say it," she said.

"What?"

"I don't know. Say whatever it is."

"I don't have anything to say. You say it."

"Why didn't you talk to Len?"

"I don't have anything to say to him."

"You could just be polite, say hello, how are you, nice weather we're having, thanks for fixing the light in my closet." She sipped her coffee and stared at me over the rim of the cup.

My hand went to the pizza, then I snatched it back. I didn't want that pizza!

"Emily — can't you accept . . . that Len is my friend?"

I looked down. "I don't know."

"Why not? Why is it so hard?"

"He's ugly," I burst out.

Mom looked like I'd slapped her. "I can't believe I heard you say that."

I couldn't speak. I felt ashamed. What I'd said was shallow and superficial. Was that me? A shallow, superficial person?

"Do you want to take it back?" Mom said. "I'm giving you a chance to take that back."

I started breathing hard. I still couldn't speak.

"You're immature," Mom said. "I didn't realize . . ."

I kept biting my lip so I wouldn't cry. How could Mom say that? I took care of the kids all the time, I cleaned the house, I shopped, I cooked supper, I did anything she asked me to

125

do. And I worked and earned money, too! "I'm responsible," I choked out.

"Yes, you're responsible. I don't deny that. But you're emotionally immature." Her voice was dry and hard."

I pushed back my chair and ran to my room. I was panting, and then I was crying. I hated what she said. I hated that she said it to me. It was as if all the things I did for her didn't mean anything. My thoughts raced. Why did I have to live here with her? I wished I was somewhere else, with my father or with Bunny, anywhere but here! Mom didn't love me anymore. I lay across my bed, willing myself to stop crying. And I did. Didn't that prove how wrong she was about me?

I heard her come into my room. I lay still. She sat on the edge of the bed and put her hand on my back. "Emily." It was hard for me not to burst into tears again. "You hurt me . . . very much . . . with your attitude." Her voice was low. Suddenly I rolled over, flung myself against her and held on, as if I were Wilma's age. I was babbling and crying. I felt so sorry. I felt so bad.

Mom stroked my hair. "I know . . . I know . . ." She held me for a long time. She kissed me. "I know you don't mean to be hurtful."

"No, no!"

"I know it . . . I know you."

126

"I'm sorry," I said. Tears again. "I won't be like that anymore. I promise."

"That's okay, don't promise anything. Just . . . be yourself. Be Emily."

She had to get ready for work. I got up and made her lunch. I wrapped her sandwich carefully. I thought about putting a note in the bag. *Dear Mom, maybe you're right about me. I'm going to grow up more. I'm going to try hard not to be emotionally immature. Love, Emily.* I didn't write the note. Instead, I put in two cookies and an apple.

Chapter 20

Every year our school goes on a picnic just before the Thanksgiving weekend. The whole school is bussed over to Indian Falls. While we were outside waiting for the buses, Robertson came over to me, took my arm and, breathing in my face, said in his excited way, "I'll see you at the picnic, Emily Beth!" He had to go on a different bus with his own class.

"Thank goodness for that," Bunny said. "He *is* a pest, isn't he?"

"Understatement of the year," I said. We got on the bus.

Bunny yawned. "I don't know why they make us do this."

Last year, we had a great time at the picnic. We horsed around and made jokes and ate so much food we were ready to burst. It was sort of your basic *cold weather, food, and games* picnic, where you hop around to keep yourself warm while you're stuffing your face, go off to play softball, then hop around some more and stuff your face some more and laugh a lot about stupid things. We loved every minute of it.

This year's picnic should have been just as good, but right away we felt it wasn't. For one thing, the food didn't seem as fabulous. Hot dogs and chips were, well, hot dogs and chips. *Not* exciting. For another thing, the weather was so warm it was more like summer than fall. And for a third thing, the whole idea of the picnic was striking Bunny and me both as just a little bit juvenile.

"I mean, what's the point?" I said, after we'd rambled around the park for a while without really getting into the picnic mood. "School spirit? We have enough of that."

"Maybe we're getting too old for this stuff," Bunny said.

I linked my arm with hers. "Look at Mr. Cooper; he hasn't put down his megaphone since we got off the bus."

We both listened to Mr. Cooper, our gym teacher, for a minute. "PLEASE DEPOSIT

TRASH IN THE BASKETS. WE DO NOT WANT TO LEAVE A BAD IMPRESSION OF OUR SCHOOL."

Bunny rolled her eyes. "Did you see him outside at the fire drill the other day? Same thing. He loooves that megaphone."

"He talks to us like we're six years old."

"I know," Bunny said. "And it's really annoying. I feel so much more mature this year. Don't you?"

"Definitely." I thought of what my mother had said about me. *Emotionally immature . . .* What if Bunny agreed? That would be awful.

Mark Shroeder came along just then and asked Bunny if she wanted to play basketball with him and some other guys. "Sure!" she said eagerly. Then she sort of backed off and looked at me. "Oh, well . . . maybe not. Emily and I — "

I gave her a shove. "Go! I'll see you later."

She went in one direction and I went in the other. I don't ever mind being alone. It gives me a chance to think about things. Sometimes, I do get sad, like when I think about my father and mother not being married anymore, but sometimes I just feel tranquil. That was how I was feeling then. I walked for a while on a footpath. Mr. Cooper's voice grew faint. The trees were all nearly bare. I stood next to a tree and tried to be as still as it was. The whole world seemed quiet and utterly peaceful.

Then I heard the thump of footsteps and, a moment later, a familiar voice. "Emily Beth!"

"What are you doing way out here, Robertson?" I said, without even turning around.

"Roaming aimlessly." He walked over to me with an innocent expression. "Imagine meeting you! What are you doing?"

"Enjoying nature."

"How do you do that?" He took out a jackknife and flipped it into the air.

"You listen to the wind in the trees. You look up in the sky. You're quiet and — " I almost screamed. "Robertson! Don't do that!" He had started carving on the trunk of the tree. "You're mutilating the tree!"

He blinked. "I just wanted to put our initials — "

"No! That tree is a living being!"

He smiled at me. "I bet you think the tree has feelings."

"What if I do?"

He grabbed me and sort of shook me back and forth. "You're so *cute*, Emily Beth." Maybe he meant to be affectionate, but he rattled my teeth! I walked fast down the path, back to the main picnic. I knew Robertson was right behind me.

"THIS IS A SCHOOL ACTIVITY," Mr. Cooper was calling through his bullhorn. "A COMMUNITY VENTURE. YOU KIDS WHO ARE

131

TENDING TO GO OFF IN PAIRS, *COME ON BACK.*"

Did he mean me . . . and *Robertson?* My whole head got hot.

"Emily Beth, Emily Beth! Want to play softball?" Robertson was at my elbow. "We can be on the same team. You want to practice your batting stance? I can give you some tips." He didn't wait for my answer, just got behind me, put his arms around me, and started breathing hard.

"Robertson!" I walked away again. He was behind me again. I walked faster. So did he. "Please don't follow me," I said.

"I'm not following you."

"What do you call it?"

"I just happen to be walking in the same direction you are, Emily Beth."

Oh. And we just happened to be talking in front of a little wooden building with a sign that said WOMEN.

I went in. When I came out, he was still hanging around. I pretended not to see him and went looking for Bunny. I found her coming off the basketball court. "Did you win?" I said.

She put her thumb and forefinger together. "What have you been doing?"

I told her about Robertson following me. "Everywhere, Bunny! I'm lucky he didn't go with me into the bathroom."

132

"That boy needs to be taught a lesson," she said. "I have an idea." She started whispering in my ear. Robertson was standing a little ways away, staring at us. "So what do you think?" she said.

"I don't know . . . do you really think it'll work?"

"What have we got to lose?" Bunny said. Then she crossed her eyes, made monkey paws, and answered herself. "Just our dignity!"

We started giggling.

"What's so funny?" Robertson called.

"Ahh! You want to know? You're curious? Come with us," Bunny said in her confident way. "We're going to take a walk." She led the way along the Red Trail down into the ravine. I was behind her, and Robertson was behind me.

"Robertson!" Bunny called over her shoulder. "You know what they say? You have to kiss a lot of frogs to find a prince. . . ."

"What?"

"YOU HAVE TO KISS A LOT OF FROGS TO FIND A PRINCE," I repeated in a loud voice. I sounded like Mr. Cooper.

"What does that mean? No, don't tell me, I can figure it out."

"Sure you can," Bunny said. "Okay, we're stopping here." She pointed to a big flat stone. "Sit down, Robertson. Emily and I want to find out if you're a prince or a frog."

He got it. He sat right down, held his face up, and looked expectantly at us.

"Is this really going to work?" I whispered to Bunny.

"Who knows," she whispered back. "Might as well try, though. We got him here!" She started mussing up Robertson's hair, really pawing her way through it. "You're *so* adorable," she shrieked, leaning herself all over him.

Robertson looked a little dazed. Before he could say anything, I joined in. I grabbed him by the ears. Bunny and I were both all over him, patting and pulling at him like he was Play-Doh, pinching his cheeks and scrubbing our hands over his face and down his shirt. "Hey, hey," he said.

Hey, hey? Our idea had been to show him what it felt like to be manhandled or, in this case, womanhandled. He was supposed to learn a lesson. He was supposed to realize that being grabbed made you feel like a *thing*, like a nonperson. He was supposed to say *Riiiight! I'll never grab again!* He wasn't supposed to sit there with a big moony smile on his face, saying, *Hey, hey!*

"Hey, hey, yourself, you adorable thing," Bunny said.

I almost died when I saw what she did next.

She got her arms around his neck and kissed him, big wet kisses all over his face. Then she rubbed his belly!

134

"Your turn," she said to me. She was breathing hard.

What could I do that was any better than what she'd done already? I kissed him, too, pressing my lips against his. But I knew everything was backfiring, because he was kissing me back enthusiastically. Any minute now, he'd say, *More, more!*

I moved away. "Forget it, Bunny. It isn't working."

I don't even know if she heard me. She flung herself at him, practically dived into his arms. She's pretty big, almost as big as Robertson, and she knocked him over, right off the rock, onto the ground. Then, I don't know who did what first, but in a blink of a second his arms were around her and hers were around him, and they were kissing. And kissing. And kissing.

"Hey!" I yelled. It was like yelling into a vacuum. They were glued together. I felt like stamping my foot. Having a temper tantrum. What did Bunny think she was doing? We were here to demonstrate to Robertson what it felt like to be mauled, to be pushed and pulled like someone's toy. We weren't here to give him a big thrill. Or *us*, either!

I walked away, feeling like the kid who'd gone to a party and had the door closed in her face. "You two are disgusting," I yelled. I waited. No answer. Didn't they hear me? I went back to tell them to their faces. And there they were, my two friends. Bunny and Robertson. My best girlfriend in the world. My other friend, my devoted *friend who was a boy*, who wanted to be *my* boyfriend. So he'd said at least twenty-five times.

I sat down under a tree and looked at them. They were *still* kissing.

Chapter 21

Right after the long Thanksgiving weekend, Dad called one night and told me he had a job interview coming up in New York City. "You're changing jobs?" I said.

"We'll see. I'm exploring possibilities." Then he casually asked if I wanted to fly down to the city for the weekend and spend some time with him. "We'll take in a couple of shows, do the big city. What do you think. Would you like that?"

Would I *like* that? No. I'd *love* that! I'd adore it! I'd kill to do it. I hadn't seen my father in nearly two years, and I really didn't quite take in what he was saying. "Is Rachel coming?" I asked. What I was thinking was that *Marcia* would be with him.

"No, I'm going alone, sweetheart. Just me. Why don't you put your mom on, and let me talk to her about it."

Just like that, he said it. So casually. *Put your mom on.* But, usually, they didn't talk much at all when he called. It was hello, good-bye, or nothing at all. I sort of caught my breath. A thought came to me. *He's breaking up with Marcia. . . . That's why he's looking for another job . . . in a different city. He's going to come back to us . . . this is the first step. . . .*

"Mom's at work, Dad." I tried to sound un-flustered. "She won't be home until midnight. I'll tell her to call you when she gets in. Oh! Unless it's too late?"

"No, that's fine. Tell Ann to call. I'll be up. I'll wait for her call."

I loved the way he said that, too! *I'll wait for her call.* After that, I was so excited I couldn't just sit still and patiently wait for Mom. When she came home, I was in the kitchen, cleaning up. I'd been baking for hours, chocolate chip cookies by the panful and a big eggy sponge cake that was Mom's favorite.

"Smells good," she said, sitting down and taking off her shoes. She massaged her neck. "I'm tired. Why are you up so late, Em?"

I poured her a cup of tea. "Dad called."

She yawned and nodded.

"He wants you to call him back."

"Why?" she said, sounding surprised.

I told her about the weekend, and then I brought her the phone. "Do you want me to dial the number?"

"Now?" she said. "I just want to go to bed and get some sleep now."

"I told him you'd call, Mom. He said it was okay for you to call as soon as you came in." I held out the phone. "I'll dial. It'll be easy. You just have to say I can come. Okay?"

"Emily, I can't just say yes."

"You're going to let me go, aren't you?!"

"Well, I have to ask your father some things."

"What things! What are you worried about? It's *Dad*."

Mom sighed. "Dial," she said. "Let's get it over with."

I swear my fingers were shaking when I dialed. A thousand things were going through my mind. Would my mother find a reason for me not to go? What if Dad had changed *his* mind about the trip? Maybe he hadn't even said it. Maybe I'd just imagined it! He answered on the first ring. "Dad? Hi! Mom's right here." I thrust the phone into her hand.

"Hello, Max." she said. She sounded sort of aloof, and she asked Dad a ton of questions — where we'd be staying, how much time I'd spend alone, what kind of clothes I needed, who was paying for all this. Did she have to say all those things? Why couldn't she just trust Dad? *Mom, be nice to him . . . be friendly . . . you know how to be sweet . . . tell him we miss him. . . .*

When she hung up, she yawned again and said, "All arranged."

"All arranged? I'm going?"

"You're going," she said with a little smile.

"Mom!" I threw my arms around her and hugged her.

Friday afternoon, Mr. Linaberry drove me to the airport after school. Mom was at the hospital. Bunny was at our house, taking care of the twins. Everything was working out perfectly, but I was in something of a trance. I couldn't believe I was going to see Dad again, at last. I kept telling myself not to fantasize, not to make up stories, but I couldn't help it. I kept imagining him saying he wanted to come back to us, that he knew he'd made a big mistake, and he was really meeting me in the city to ask me — no, to BEG me — to talk to Mom, to smooth the way for him to return to us. Us, his real family.

"Here's your airline," Mr. Linaberry said, stopping the truck in front of the building.

I picked up my knapsack and glanced at my watch.

"Plenty of time," he said.

I opened the door and started to get out, then I realized I hadn't thanked him. It was a half-hour drive from home to the airport, and I hadn't said a single word to him the whole way. I'd been all wrapped up in my fantasies about my father. Mom's words came back again. *Emotionally immature*. Wouldn't I ever forget that?

I slid back into the truck, balancing on the edge of the high seat with my legs dangling. "Thank you for the ride, Mr. Linaberry."

"That's okay."

I felt that I should say something else. "I really really appreciate you taking me here."

"That's okay."

He wasn't looking at me. Did he hate me? Did he think I was a spoiled brat? Emotionally immature? I bit my lip. What else could I say to him? I couldn't be a hypocrite and say, I love you, or anything like that. And I certainly couldn't tell him I was sorry I'd called him ugly! If I was lucky, he'd never know about that.

I said, "Would you tell Wilma and Chris I'm going to bring them back something from New York City? I forgot to say it."

"Sure, sure."

"I thought it might make them feel a little better about not seeing Dad if they know I'm going to bring them something," I explained.

Mr. Linaberry nodded.

It seemed to me that by telling him all this, I

was letting him know I was trying to accept that he was Mom's friend. Of course, if Dad came back to us, Mr. Linaberry could never be anything else but a friend. *Oh, please,* I prayed again. And suddenly I felt totally light, almost weightless, and a feeling of happiness spread through me, as if I knew *for sure* my message had flown across the country and lodged in Dad's heart.

"I'll bring you something, too, Mr. Linaberry," I said impulsively. I was so full of an extraordinary happiness in that moment I just wanted to spread it out, share it.

"Me?"

"What would you like?"

He thought about it. "Maybe a pencil that says, 'New York City, the Big Apple.'"

"Okay."

"Or a Statue of Liberty T-shirt."

"Okay."

"I'd like that," he said.

"Okay," I said again. It was probably the best conversation Mr. Linaberry and I had ever had.

When I got on the plane, I took out my journal to write. "With all my dreaming about Dad, I hardly gave one thought to Wilma and Chris. I realized this when I was talking to Mr. Linaberry after he brought me to the airport. I always thought I was so mature and unselfish. It seems like most of the time, though, I'm thinking about myself. I want to be be more mature. I'm going to try much harder to be more considerate to-ward other people, and be more serious and down to earth and mature."

It made me feel better to write that.

The steward brought around drinks, and peanuts in a little silver bag. I sipped my soda and looked out the window. In just twenty minutes, I'd see Dad again. We'd talk and make plans. We'd be closer than ever. What if he said Marcia would be so hurt by his leaving her? I'd point out that they hadn't even been married three years, so it wouldn't be anything near as horrible as when he and Mom split up. It had to hurt a lot more the longer you were married. Then I thought about my half sister, Rachel. Maybe I would suggest to Dad that Marcia and Rachel move east, too, so he could see the baby sometimes. Even if she was too young to understand what was happening, I didn't want Rachel to go through what we had gone through.

The plane landed at La Guardia with a thump, and my heart thumped, too, with a sudden scary thought. What if I didn't recognize my father after all this time? I walked through the long tunnel filled with people holding briefcases and flight bags. In the gate area, I searched the crowds for Dad. I didn't see him anywhere and, in a panic, I put on my glasses as I started walking toward the main terminal.

Dad was waiting right outside the security gate

143

in a crowd of people. I saw him before he saw me, and for a split second it was like looking at a stranger. He was wearing a dark suit, a striped tie and a striped shirt, and he looked like someone impressive and serious. Not like my father, who was always full of fun.

I walked toward him fast, my knapsack over one shoulder, bumping against me. "Dad," I called. "Dad, Dad!"

"Emily — !" He stepped toward me.

I'd forgotten that he stooped a little, as if he were always on the verge of stepping through a door that wasn't quite high enough. I'd forgotten that his hairline was receding, and that he showed a high curved forehead. How could I have forgotten so much? How could I have forgotten even one tiny detail about him? My eyes filled, I dropped my knapsack, and threw my arms around him.

Chapter 22

"Bunny, hi! Are you awake? Did I call too early?"

"At noon? You know I never sleep 'til noon."

"So take a guess where I'm calling you from."

"A phone booth on the street. I can hear the car horns and sirens."

"Wrong."

"A cellular phone in a taxi."

"Wrong! I'm in the hotel. In our room. You can hear all that stuff even though the windows are closed and we're on the sixteenth floor."

"What are you doing? What have you done? Is it exciting being there? Tell me everything."

"Last night, after Dad met me at the plane, we took a taxi to the hotel. He was already checked in, so we just went up, and I unpacked.

We ate supper and then we went to a movie. Right now, I'm waiting for Dad to come back from his meeting. He was gone when I woke up. The first thing I did was take a shower — "

"Emily. Emily! You don't have to tell me every detail."

"You said for me to tell you everything."

"Right, but I didn't mean *everything*. Just give me the important stuff."

"I have to tell you this, Bunny. It's a luxury hotel. There's a basket in the bathroom with tiny fancy bottles of shampoo and three different kinds of hand-milled soap. There's a big fluffy white bathrobe to put on after your shower. Plus a hair dryer, remote control TV, of course, and a tiny refrigerator full of snacks."

"What kind of snacks?"

"I knew you'd like that. Chocolate, crackers, sodas, little bottles of juice. A bar of chocolate is four dollars. Everything is unbelievably expensive. Did I say we ate in the hotel dining room last night? It's beautiful. The tablecloths and napkins are pink linen. There're flowers on every table. A waiter in a black tux took our order. Guess what Dad's baked potato cost? Three dollars! Last week I bought Mom ten pounds of potatoes in the market, and I didn't pay half that much."

"Was the food good?"

"Delicious! Dad's trying to lose weight. He

had shrimp cocktail, baked potato, and some kind of grilled fish. Red snapper, I think. I had baby lamb chops with mint jelly and chocolate cake for dessert. I don't want to even tell you how much the whole thing cost."

"Were the baby lamb chops wearing little diapers? Sorry, I couldn't resist. Are we through with last night? Have you done anything exciting this morning?"

"I ate breakfast in a croissant shop. I walked around for hours. I experienced New York. Park Avenue. Lexington Avenue. Fifth Avenue. They're fabulous. Dad said if I stayed around the streets near the hotel, I would be okay. You wouldn't believe the things you see in the stores here."

"Did you buy anything?"

"I just window-shopped. I didn't have the nerve to go in anywhere."

"Emily, they don't charge you for walking into a store. You've got to go in. When I was in New York with Mom last year, half the fun was shopping."

"Well, you're just more sophisticated than I am."

"True."

"I think I'm running out of things to tell you."

"Okay, I'll tell you something. Our mutual friend called me last night."

"Robertson?"

"Yes. He's madly madly in love with me."

"That's what he said?"

"Aren't you glad his Emily fever is gone?"

"What else did he say?"

"Oh, this and that. He just about wants to run away with me."

"Did he tell you you were beautiful and adorable and cute?"

"Emily, I thought I was bringing you good news. I thought I'd hear a rousing cheer and that there'd be a big celebration. The pest is out of your life at last!"

"Well . . . he wasn't *that* much of a pest."

"Are you telling me you care, Emily? I thought Robbie was just one big pain to you."

"*Robbie?*"

"That's what I call him . . . Emily, are you jealous?"

"Nooo! But I didn't exactly hate the guy, Bunny."

"Don't worry, you're still his friend. That's probably much better than being the object of his overwhelming affections."

"How *much* do you like him?"

"Hmmmm. He's a cute kid, and he knows how to kiss. But it is kind of embarrassing to like someone twelve years old!"

"Tell me about it."

"Yeah . . . that's the thing."

"How much have you kissed him?"

"Hold on there. I just saw him at the picnic. You know what happened there. . . ."

"Yes . . ."

"I couldn't help myself. It was a case of instant insanity."

I had to laugh. "You're crazy."

"That's what I just said. Oh, my mother's calling me. I gotta hang up now, Emily. Love ya!"

"Me, too. 'Bye."

" 'Bye-bye!"

That afternoon, Dad and I went to a museum, another movie, and F.A.O. Schwarz, a really great toy store, to find presents for Wilma and Chris. "I don't know how we're doing so much," Dad said. He tucked my arm through his. "We're terrific, Emily. We're taking this city by storm."

We had so much fun. Everything we did was fun. I hoped I would never forget a single thing. I promised myself as soon as we got back to the hotel I'd write everything down in my journal. The only thing I didn't like was that we were so busy we didn't get to really talk.

We ate supper in a Mexican restaurant. The walls had bright murals of Mexico painted on them. There were candles on the tables and mariachi music playing in the background. The food was better than any Mexican food I'd ever tasted.

We started talking about the twins, and I told Dad how Chris took his Original Disappearing Snowman paperweight everywhere.

"He really likes it." Dad looked pleased.

"He'd like anything that came from you," I said. Then I told him some Wilma stories.

Dad really laughed. "She's something else. She's a pistol! That girl is always going to be okay; she'll know how to take care of herself. By the way, Emily — "

Everytime he said *by the way* . . . I got a tight feeling in my chest, and I thought about him coming back to us. "Yes, Dad?" Was he going to say it now? Under the table, I crossed my fingers. I looked at him, his eyes, his broad shining forehead and big bony shoulders. I loved him so much.

"I just realized, with all our shopping, we didn't get you anything today. We should have bought something for you in the museum shop."

"I don't want anything. I'm here this weekend. That's my present."

"Are you sure? Don't you want anything at all?"

My heart gave that plane-landing *thump*. Yes, there was something I wanted! I looked down at my plate. In the scraps of food, in the bits of tortilla and shreds of lettuce on my plate, I suddenly saw the letters H and R. H for Home. R for Return. I looked up. "Dad, are you ever coming back?"

"What? Back?" A startled, unhappy look crossed his face.

"I want you to come home," I said.

"Emily. Emily. This was settled long ago. That's not my home anymore. Your mom and I aren't — "

"It's not right for me not to have a father." My eyes were wet.

"You do have a father."

"Far away! I never see you. It's not fair."

"I know how you feel, honey. Don't you think I wish I could see more of you, too? I love seeing you. I wish I didn't live so far away."

"Why did you go there? You shouldn't have gone there."

"You know why, for a better job. And if I come to New York City, it'll be for a better job, too." He put his hand over mine. "It's been a great weekend so far, honey. We've had fun, we've done a lot together, and it isn't over yet." I nodded and sank down in my seat. I wished I was home. I didn't want to be here anymore. I didn't want to even look at Dad. I told myself I had to act mature, and I forced out a smile. Why did I feel this way? What was the matter with me? In my mind, my *sensible* mind, my *emotionally mature* mind, hadn't I always known he wasn't coming back?

"You okay?" he said.

"Sure. I'm fine." My throat felt sore and I drank some water.

Dad pushed aside his plate and took a picture from his wallet. "Look, I brought this for you. Here's your sister Rachel." My eyes were blurry and I could barely see the picture. A little girl with curly blonde hair and tiny white teeth. "I think she looks a lot like you," Dad said.

Why would he say that? I had dark straight hair and so did Wilma and Chris. He handed me another picture of Rachel, this one with Marcia holding her in her lap. I held it near the candle to see it better. I held it so close it suddenly caught fire. I froze. I didn't drop the picture. I watched the blue and yellow flames race to my fingers.

Dad threw water over my hand. A hissing sound. The picture was ruined, curled and blackened. "Sorry," I whispered. My face felt hotter than the tips of my fingers where the flames had touched them. Dad dropped his napkin over the mess on the table. "Are you okay? Let me see your hand."

I shook my head. "It's okay." I kept my hand in my lap.

Dessert came, a cool pudding sort of thing.

We were sort of awkward. Dad tried to keep things light. He told me a funny story about how hard it was to live in Chicago and be a Boston Red Sox fan. I laughed politely. It wasn't until later, when I was in bed, that I let myself think about what Dad had said before I burned the picture, and what it meant. He was never going to come back to us. Never.

Chapter 23

Sunday morning, while we were having breakfast, Dad said he had a longing to see the ocean again. "I want to see it and smell it. How about you?"

I shrugged.

"What does that mean?" Dad said. "Is that indifference or agreement?"

"It means if you want to go to the ocean, it's okay with me."

"I don't want to do something you won't enjoy."

I shrugged again.

Dad looked at me with a little smile. "Emmy — come back."

"I'm right here," I said, but I knew what he

154

meant. Since last night I felt sort of cool and removed.

We put on jeans and sweatshirts, and we took the subway, a long ride, over an hour, out to Coney Island. I didn't feel like talking, but Dad kept a conversation of sorts going. "I know you've been to the ocean before, Emmy, but not Coney Island. Coney Island is special. Too bad we're going this time of year."

"The water will still be there," I said.

"Yes, but in the right season there'd be music, we could eat the famous Nathan's hot dogs, and take a ride on the loop-the-loop, and the board-walk would be crowded with thousands of people. Thousands!" His eyes sparkled.

When we finally got there, there weren't thousands but there were quite a lot of people, old people mostly, sitting on the benches along the boardwalk. I thought it was beautiful. Below us, the sand stretched for what seemed like miles. The sky was pale and there was a blurred sun behind a ripple of clouds. The wind was blow-ing, and I zipped up my sweatshirt as we walked down the steps and over the sand toward the water. From a distance, the sand had looked smooth, but walking on it, I saw that it was full of bits of shells and plastic and chunks of glass.

And it wasn't as empty as I'd thought at first, either. A girl and a boy, standing in the middle of the beach, looking like a poster for a movie, were kissing passionately. A man was fishing, and a bunch of kids were playing on the big finger rocks that reached out into the ocean. Dad and I walked along the edge of the water. I turned around to look at the Ferris wheel and the roller coaster behind us. They looked black and sort of bony against the sky. I wished I had my journal with me to write that down.

"Great, isn't it?" Dad said. All of a sudden he took off running. He ran a little distance, turned, and came running back, whooping and panting. Just as he came close to me, he picked up something from the sand. "Hey, look what I found!" He grinned and held it up. It was a green plastic water gun. "It must have washed in. Fruits of the sea!" He handed it to me.

I was going to put it in my pocket and give it to Wilma. But suddenly I bent over, filled it with water and aimed at Dad. A jet of water hit him in the arm. I shot again and got him in the chest. "Emily!" I didn't stop. I was squirting him, shooting him. I shot again and got him full in the face. And again and again.

"You're going to pay for this," he said, ducking and covering his face.

The fingers I'd burned last night started to tingle. I dropped the gun and walked away. What did he mean, *pay?* What would he do? Go away? Leave me here on the beach? Walk away from me and never look back? *I don't care. Let him go!* I looked over my shoulder. Dad was coming after me, waving for me to wait for him. Instead, I started running, running really hard. The wind was in my hair, I picked up my feet and let them slap down on the sand. *I don't care . . . I don't care . . . I don't care. . . .* My feet pounded to that rhythm.

Then I heard Dad calling me again, and I looked back. He was bent over, kneeling on the sand, his head down, as if he'd collapsed. I turned, skidded in the sand, half fell. I ran. *Oh, please . . .* I was praying again. *I do care . . . I do care . . .* When I got to him, he was brushing off his knees, and he looked chagrined, not sick. "Dad?" I said.

"I got out of breath running after you. Stupid." He sat down on the sand, and I sat down beside him. The sand was cold through my jeans.

"Dad, you're out of shape," I said.

"I know, I know." He handed me the water gun. "Don't you want to bring it to Chris?"

"Chris hates guns. Wilma will like it better."

"Wilma . . ." he said musingly. "Yeah, I can see it. I wonder if Rachel will be like her. Or you? You're all so different. You, you were always looking, from the time you were a little thing. Your mother and I used to joke that you were taking notes on the world."

"What else?" I wanted him to remember more about me.

"Let me think. Oh, yes, the way you talked, that was something. You could say anything. Any big word, you'd just repeat it." He put his hand on my shoulder.

It was just a touch, my father's touch, my father's hand on my shoulder, nothing unusual, but it brought me a kind of revelation. Maybe it was the sun that did it, the dazzle of light on the water clearing out my mind. Or maybe it was just that warm, ordinary touch of his hand. Because, right then, I knew with a kind of pure certainty that, even if Dad didn't think of us as much as we wanted him to, even if he forgot to call us and write us, even if he was away from us, no matter where he was, he was still and always our father. And we were his children, and nothing could take that away from us. Nothing could change that.

I leaned back, leaned against him, and he put his arm around me and kissed my hair. "Emmy," he said. Then we sat there for a while, looking out at the bright metallic water.

Chapter 24

"It was great, just great," I said. "New York was great. I definitely want to go there again."

"I don't see that you did so much that was different," Bunny said. She was sitting cross-legged on her bed. "You saw a movie. You can see movies here."

"Two movies," I corrected her. "Plus the museum, plus Coney Island, plus fabulous window-shopping, and Mexican food, and the hotel — "

"Hold it, Em, I just heard the bell downstairs." She got up. "I'll be right back."

I lay back on her bed with my hands behind my head. I heard voices downstairs. Bunny's voice. And then another voice. I sat up. A voice I recognized.

159

"I really like that you're so tall," I heard Robertson saying as I went down the stairs. "I admire a tall girl."

Bunny laughed. "You make it sound like a talent."

"If you think about it logically, it is a talent, something given to you that you use. You've been given height and you use it to play great basketball. When I see you striding around the halls in school, I say to myself, 'Robertson, that girl stands tall!' "

I went into the front hall. "Hi, Robertson," I said.

"Emily!" He looked a little shocked.

"It's me, your very own true love."

"What are you doing here?" he said, which was not the brightest question in the world, especially for a bright boy like Robertson.

"Visiting my friend, Bunny Larrabee. I take it you're doing the same. I heard you were busy while I was in New York. As busy as a little boy bee can be busy."

Robertson got an injured look on his big face. "Hey, hey, hey, Emily, what's all that sarcasm about?"

"Sarcasm, Robertson? I'll get to the point. What about you and Bunny? I heard something was going on."

"What?" he said. "What? Nothing's going on."

160

"Nothing? Oh, wait a *second*," Bunny protested.

"I heard that you love her."

Bunny nodded.

"And that you're through with me."

Bunny nodded again.

"I still like you, Emily."

"Not much," I said.

"No! A lot."

"A lot?" Bunny said. "What about me? I thought I was the one now. You better explain yourself, Robertson."

He looked from me to Bunny. From Bunny to me. "Both of you," he said.

"Both of us? Emily, this boy is greedy! I think we need a conference, don't you?"

She gave me an elbow in the side, and I said, "Absolutely right. Robertson, you wait here. Bunny and I are going to have a conference."

We left him in the hall and went into the kitchen and closed the door. "What are we going to do?" I said.

"Teach him a lesson."

"We already tried that, Bunny, remember? We didn't have much success last time. Maybe we should just tell him to choose one of us."

"I don't like that. It gives him too much power. Why should *he* choose *us*? Why don't we get to make the decision? Besides, if he chooses me, you're going to feel slighted, and it's going to hurt our friendship."

"What if he chooses *me*?" I said. "Are you going to feel slighted and hurt our friendship?"

"I refuse to be jealous of my best friend."

"Me, too!"

"Good. Now the next question is, which one of us does he get? Oops, I mean, which one of us gets him?"

"Wait a second," I said. "Before we answer that question, we should decide if we even want him for a boyfriend."

"You're right!" Bunny said. "Do you want him?"

I thought about it, then I shook my head. Robertson was nice when you could keep him on a leash, sort of rein him in. But that was too much work and not my idea of the way to have a boyfriend.

"I don't actually want him, either," Bunny confessed. "I just liked the novelty of it. And he is rather adorable and handsome."

"Mmm, his eyes," I said.

"Mmm, his lips," Bunny said.

Which gave us the idea for our plan. It didn't seem too original to me, but Bunny's brother, Shad, came in, and the plan got better.

Shad was carrying his pet parakeet in the crook of his arm. The bird chirped, and Shad gave it a kiss on the bill. I think Bunny and I both had the same idea at the same moment. We sort of interrupted each other explaining to Shad what we wanted.

"No, thanks," he said. He stroked his parakeet's back.

"Do it for me," Bunny said. "Do it for your sister. Where's your family loyalty?"

"No, thanks."

"Emily will kiss you as a reward," Bunny said. That came as news to me.

Shad looked at me and blushed. "You will?"

"Uh, sure."

"You don't have to, Emily," Shad said. "I'll help you out, anyway."

"I knew you would! You're a good kid!" Bunny gave her brother a smart slap on the back, then we went out into the front hall.

Robertson was leaning against the wall, whistling through his cupped hand. "Patiently waiting," he said. "Have you finished your conference?"

"Yes, and we're going to give you a test," Bunny said. "We're going to test your powers of, of — " She looked at me.

" — discrimination," I supplied.

Bunny nodded. "You may not think this is too original, Robbie, but this also involves kissing."

Robertson smiled.

"First, we blindfold you." Bunny tied a dishcloth around his eyes and whirled him around.

"Now, concentrate, Robbie. You've got to guess who is kissing you in what order. Got that?"

"Got it." His smile was even bigger.

Bunny pointed at me. I stood on tiptoes and gave him a strong kiss. Bunny whirled him again. I kissed him again, more softly this time. By then Shad had tiptoed in. Bunny pointed at him, and he touched his lips to Robertson's and tiptoed out. Once again, she whirled him around. Then she kissed him three times in a row.

After that, we took the dishcloth off his eyes.

"Now you have to say which one of us kissed you and in what order," Bunny said. "This is classic, Robbie. We find out who's your true love this way, because true love recognizes true love's kiss."

"You want to do it again, so I can really concentrate?" he asked.

"Sorry."

"What happens if I fail this test?"

"You lose both of us."

"No problem, anyway, because I know," he said, with his usual confidence. "First time, it was Bunny."

"Okay. Then who?"

"Emily."

"Then who?"

"Bunny again, two more times." He thought

for a minute. "There were six kisses. It was Emily, the last two times."

"Let me get this straight," Bunny said. "Me, Emily, me, me, Emily, Emily?"

"Right," Robertson said.

"Wrong," Bunny said. "It went like *this*. Emily, Emily, Shad, me, me, me."

"Shad?" he said.

"My brother. Didn't you ever hear, Love me, love my brother?"

"Your brother kissed me?"

"He didn't do it willingly," Bunny admitted.

Robertson wiped his hand across his mouth. "You're kidding me, aren't you?"

I shook my head.

"Scouts' honor," Bunny said, and we both raised our hands in our old three-fingered Girl Scout salute.

After that, we walked Robertson to the corner, one on each side of him. "This is the last mile, Robbie," Bunny said. "It's kind of sad, isn't it?"

"The passing of an epoch," I said. "The epoch of Robertson."

"I really didn't pass?" he said.

"No, you didn't."

"So what does it mean?"

"What it means, Robbie, as I told you before," Bunny explained kindly, "is that you can't have either of us."

"Neither of you?" he said weakly.

"But you can be a friend to both of us. You can come to us for help with your other girlfriends."

"I don't have any other girlfriends."

"Well, we're sure you'll have someone before long." We were at the corner. "This is as far as we go with you," Bunny said.

Robertson walked a few steps, then looked back at us. "Don't you think it was cheating to include Shad?"

"Yeah, probably," Bunny admitted. "Sorry about that."

He walked a few more steps, then turned again. "Are you absolutely sure you want to do this? I can't understand it. Don't you like me?"

"He sounds so pathetic," Bunny whispered.

"I know, it's sad."

We looked at each other, then we ran up to him and threw our arms around him. "We'll always love you, Robertson," I said.

"We'll never forget you, Seventh Grade Lover," Bunny said. "And don't forget, we're going to be in your life, to give you good advice about your next girlfriend."

"You really think I'll get another girlfriend?"

"It's guaranteed," I said.

We watched him walk away. He seemed to straighten up and sort of hop and skip along as if he were having happier and happier thoughts.

When we went back to Bunny's house, Shad was taking his bike out of the garage. "I'm gonna collect, Emily," he said.

"I thought you helped us out of the goodness of your heart."

"I changed my mind," he yelled, getting on his bike."

"Great," I said, looking at Bunny. "At this rate, I might hit it lucky and have a three-year-old boyfriend by summertime."

Bunny just laughed.

About the Author

NORMA FOX MAZER is the author of more than twenty books for young readers, among them the Newbery honor winner *After the Rain*, as well as *Taking Terri Mueller*, *When We First Met*, and *Downtown*. Ms. Mazer has twice won the Lewis Carroll Shelf Award; she has also won the California Young Reader Medal and has been nominated for the National Book Award.

E, My Name Is Emily is a companion book to *A, My Name Is Ami*; *B, My Name Is Bunny*; *C, My Name Is Cal*; and *D, My Name is Danita*, all published by Scholastic.

Ms. Mazer lives with her husband, author Harry Mazer, in the Pompey Hills outside Syracuse, New York.

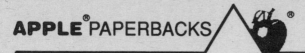

APPLE® PAERBACKS

Pick an Apple and Polish Off Some Great Reading!

BEST-SELLING APPLE TITLES

❏ MT43944-8 **Afternoon of the Elves** Janet Taylor Lisle — $2.75

❏ MT43109-9 **Boys Are Yucko** Anna Grossnickle Hines — $2.95

❏ MT43473-X **The Broccoli Tapes** Jan Slepian — $2.95

❏ MT40961-1 **Chocolate Covered Ants** Stephen Manes — $2.95

❏ MT45436-6 **Cousins** Virginia Hamilton — $2.95

❏ MT44036-5 **George Washington's Socks** Elvira Woodruff — $2.95

❏ MT45244-4 **Ghost Cadet** Elaine Marie Alphin — $2.95

❏ MT44351-8 **Help! I'm a Prisoner in the Library** Eth Clifford — $2.95

❏ MT43618-X **Me and Katie (The Pest)** Ann M. Martin — $2.95

❏ MT43030-0 **Shoebag** Mary James — $2.95

❏ MT46075-7 **Sixth Grade Secrets** Louis Sachar — $2.95

❏ MT42882-9 **Sixth Grade Sleepover** Eve Bunting — $2.95

❏ MT41732-0 **Too Many Murphys** Colleen O'Shaughnessy McKenna — $2.95

Available wherever you buy books, or use this order form.

Scholastic Inc., P.O. Box 7502, 2931 East McCarty Street, Jefferson City, MO 65102

Please send me the books I have checked above. I am enclosing $_____ (please add $2.00 to cover shipping and handling). Send check or money order — no cash or C.O.D.s please.

Name_____ Birthdate_____

Address _____

City_____ State/Zip _____

Please allow four to six weeks for delivery. Offer good in the U.S.A. only. Sorry, mail orders are not available to residents of Canada. Prices subject to change.

APP693